Cabaret of the Dead

A Novelization of the Zombie-Comedy Film

Written by
STACI   LAYNE   WILSON

Author's Other Books (Select Bibliography)

Series:
Rock & Roll Nightmares
Immortal Confessions

Novels:
Rock N Roll Fantasy
The Tragedy Man

Short Story Collection:
City of Devils

Memoir:
So L.A.

PRAISE FOR CABARET OF THE DEAD

"Burlesque on roller skates, eyeball-munching zombies, and aliens who speak in B-movie lines--in other words, another incredibly fun read from the mind of Staci Layne Wilson!"
Deborah Brock, director of *Slumber Party Massacre II* (1987)

"Staci Layne Wilson paints a perfect picture of the hidden-in-plain-sight Los Angeles nightlife while giving the reader a remarkable glimpse behind the speakeasy password-protected world of fetish performers. If that were all... that would be more than enough. But there are also zombies! And in a world where we've seen every variation of the genre, Wilson throws twists I didn't see coming. And if that's not enough... 'vision of vintage vixen bewitchery, boasting a bullet bra...' her alliteration game is next level!"
Todd Farmer, screenwriter of *Jason X* (2001)

"With fantastic female characters, callbacks to classic horror films, and a cheeky approach to dealing with pesky zombies, *Cabaret of the Dead* perfectly balances scares with smiles."
Barbara Magnolfi, 'Olga' in *Suspiria* (1977)

Table of Contents:

Part One: Showgirls, page 6
Part Two: All That Jazz, 46
Part Three: Zombies Vs. Strippers, 87
Part Four: From Dusk Till Dawn, 137

Chapter 1

On a bustling, clear evening in Hollywood, the streets pulse with life. A colorful weave of tourists, locals, vagabonds, eccentrics, trendsetters, and influencers parade along the star-studded boulevard.

In a whirlwind of activity, iconic landmarks flash by in quick succession—the renowned eateries like Miceli's, Musso and Frank, the Pig & Whistle, and Mel's Drive-In. Old haunts, steeped in history, beckon with their tarnished allure, from The Frolic Room to Boardner's. Glittering theaters such as The Egyptian, The Pantages, and The Chinese stand proud, while the Hollywood Roosevelt exudes timeless glamour. Even Ripley's Believe It or Not adds its peculiar charm to the mix.

Under a darkening blue sky and from the lofty heights of the Hollywood and Highland complex, a scene unfolds—a bustling mosaic of traffic lights, scooter riders, and gridlocked vehicles. An urban symphony fills the air with the blare of horns, the thumping bass of radios, and voices carried on the faint wind. Among the throngs of pedestrians, there's a kaleidoscope of humanity, from curious onlookers to casual window-shoppers and wide-eyed tourists, their dreams encapsulated in snapshots with aging superheroes and retro glam icons.

And there she is, amidst the swirl of activity: a woman sporting shoulder-length blonde locks and a figure that effortlessly straddles the line between slender and curvaceous. Clad in snug jeans and a tight, artistically torn *Star Wars* tee, she exudes a youthful vibrancy, her face aglow with an unmistakable freshness. White earbuds dangling, she strolls past the iconic Chinese Theater, a fleeting yet captivating presence in the glittering set-piece of Hollywood's oncoming nocturnal magic.

Her name is Bettie—well, not really. That's just what she's called at The Fetish Factory, her nighttime workplace. She loves it there. Movie nerd that she is, she's always thought of it as *Night Shift* meets *Showgirls*. Later, when it turned into *Night Shift* meets *Showgirls* meets *Re-Animator*, she didn't like it so much anymore. But for now, Bettie is blissfully unaware of the horror that awaits her.

She shifts her gaze from the Hollywood and Highland balcony walkway and continues her purposeful course. She's got the thousand-yard stare of a gorgeous girl in a cesspool of potential perverts. Earbuds now firmly in place, she's listening to her tunes and her demeanor is one of a Hollywood local—she doesn't look at anyone, she doesn't read the names on the sidewalk stars upon which she steps, and she doesn't rubberneck at the sales signage.

But she can't ignore it when a disheveled bible-thumper comes out of nowhere and blocks her path.

"Sinner! Harlot! You are doomed. Doooomed, I say!" The thin, scraggly woman raises her hands to the sky and mumbles, "And after these things, I saw four angels standing on the four corners of the earth, holding the four winds of the earth."

I'm no angel, Bettie thinks.

Getting no response from Bettie, the woman wanders off in search of her next potential disciple.

Bettie sees her vintage 1970 dark green Mercedes Benz 280 SL roadster down the block and prays there's no parking ticket on it today. But it's the bleak, black heart of Hollywood, so of course there's a parking ticket. She crumples it up and tosses it into the glovebox where it joins its overpriced brethren.

She drives the short distance to Lincoln Heights, where tonight's Fetish Factory is set up.

Irma told her to look for an old, fancy, white, three-story house. That's a bit different—the show usually pops up in black box theaters, rooftop party spaces, or small warehouses.

As she rounds the corner of 110 Downey Avenue in the rundown 'hood, she finds herself staring at a relic from another era: the Horace B. Dibble House. Its imposing presence looms against the backdrop of a crisp dusk, its Victorian Queen Anne architecture standing proud and defiant. The air is heavy with the scent of roses, their pink blooms adding an unexpected touch of delicacy to the scene.

The house is a study in contrasts. Intricate woodwork adorns its façade, evidence of the careful craftsmanship of a bygone era. The bay window juts out like a watchful eye, its panes reflecting the flickering light of distant lightning. A distinctive gabled roof reaches toward the heavens, its peaks cutting sharp lines against the darkening sky. A rustic red fence encircles the property, its paint chipped and weather-worn.

But for all its grandeur, there is an undeniable sense of decay. The wood, once rich and painted a gleaming white, now bears the weathered marks of time's passage. The front porch sags slightly as if weary from years of bearing witness to the secrets held within. As Bettie draws nearer, she notices the details that make the Dibble House truly unique. Decorative trims adorn its façade, intricate patterns etched into the wood like hieroglyphs from a forgotten language.

Despite the beauty of its surroundings, there is something undeniably unsettling about the house. It sits. Brooding. A silent sentinel guarding its secrets from prying eyes. And as she stands before it, she can't shake the feeling that she is being watched, that the house itself is alive with a presence all its own.

Bettie kills the engine of her Mercedes, the soft purr of the car giving way to the cacophony of a storm brewing above. She steps out into the night, her boots clicking on the pavement as she pulls a cover over her precious vehicle. She secures it against the wind that's picking up, tugging at her hair and clothes like an insistent child.

The path to the front porch is narrow, flanked by overgrown bushes that brush against her jeans, leaving dewy kisses on the denim. There it is, The Fetish Factory's calling card—a neon high-heeled pump shoe—casting a lurid pink glow over the entrance. It flickers in and out of life, battling against the encroaching darkness. Bettie can't help but smirk at its brazenness; even in a place as somber as this old house, a bit of risqué fun refuses to be stifled.

She climbs the steps to the porch, each creak of wood beneath her feet telling tales of olden days. The shoe's phosphorescent glow paints her face in shades of fuchsia, lending an otherworldly look to her features. For a moment, she imagines herself as a noir heroine—steely-eyed and fearless—about to uncover mysteries in an old Hollywood flick.

She knocks in The Fetish Factory's coded "Shave and haircut, two bits" pattern, and a small sliding opening in the door reveals just a slice of a dark-skinned man's glowering face.

"Password?" he demands.

Bettie chuckles. "Go fuck yourself."

"Yeah, yeah," he says, grinning as he opens the door. "Entres, mi'lady."

As she slips past The Gatekeeper, he towers over her menacingly, then gives her a wink. "Have a nice night, Bettie."

She steps tentatively over the threshold, her heart pounding with a mixture of excitement and trepidation. The old, creaky floorboards beneath her feet seem to groan in protest as she enters, echoing the house's age and wear. The scent of dust and old wood fills her nostrils, mingling with the faint aroma of stale cigarette smoke and cologne. She shivers as the wind outside begins to howl. *This is what I get for watching The House on Haunted Hill before bed last night*, she thinks.

Her eyes widen in wonder as she takes in the sight before her. This is way cooler than a black box theater or a warehouse. To her right, the stage room beckons, bathed in the warm glow of dimmed lights. Marshall stack amps stand sentinel on the platform, their presence lending an air of rock 'n roll rebellion to the otherwise opulent surroundings. Assorted chairs are arranged haphazardly around the room, their plush cushions inviting patrons to linger and watch the whole show. A small, fully stocked bar glistens in the far corner, promising liquid courage to performers and audience alike.

To her left, a stairway leads upwards, disappearing into the shadows above. Bettie's curiosity tugs at her, urging her to explore further, but she resists, knowing she has little time to spare. Instead, she turns her attention straight ahead, where the dressing room awaits.

As she enters, her eyes light up with delight at the sight of the alluring costumes hanging from a rolling wardrobe rack. Each garment seems more extravagant than the last, dripping with sequins and feathers in a riot of color. A makeup vanity sits in the corner, its light-bulb-dotted mirror casting a flattering glow on Bettie's reflection. Perfume bottles, makeup palettes, and feather boas clutter its surface, a testament to the meticulous preparations that go into creating the perfect burlesque persona. Clinging to the walls are vintage mannequins, headless dress forms, and black, red, and silver garments festooned with sequins, fringe, and fishnet. High-heeled shoes in various sizes lie in a pile in a dark corner.

Just beyond the dressing room, she spots the manager's office, its door slightly ajar. Intrigued, she pushes it open and steps inside, gasping in awe at the sight before her. The walls are adorned with framed paintings of luscious ladies, their curves immortalized in strokes of vibrant color against the wood-paneled backdrop. A red velvet settee and a leopard-print sofa beckon, their plush cushions inviting Bettie to sink into their embrace. A 1950s atomic-age coffee table sits in the center of the room, its sleek lines a stark contrast to the opulent surroundings. She wonders where the bosses are—clearly, they've been here, bringing in the costumes and setting up, but it's not like them to make themselves scarce before a show. She notices three doors, wondering where each leads, and suspects that the architect must've been a maze-maker in his spare time. She leaves the room and returns to the girls' digs.

Bettie takes off her street clothes—the *Star Wars* shirt, which has a silkscreened portrait of Han Solo with the words "I know" above, was a thrift store find and is her current fave—and dons a vintage silk robe. With a determined smile, she sets about the task of gathering the pieces of her costume, knowing that showtime waits for no one. Bettie's fingers deftly maneuver the tubes and compacts of makeup, her movements practiced and precise. With each stroke of lipstick, each sweep of eyeliner, she sheds the skin of her everyday self and emerges anew, transformed into a vision of vintage allure. The modern world fades away as she immerses herself in the ritual of becoming someone else, someone bold and brazen, with fire-engine red lips that could tempt even the most steadfast of souls. The black Bettie Page wig is the final touch, its sleek waves cascading around her face like a veil of mystery. With it, she sheds her identity and steps into the shoes of yesterday's temptress, ready to command the stage with her every move. The bangs are slightly askew, but it'll have to do for now.

Just as she settles into her transformation, the room is suddenly filled with a rush of air, the force of an adjacent door bursting open. Startled, Bettie turns, her leopard-print robe billowing around her semi-nude form. She peers out the dressing room window and sees a squall raging overhead, casting the yard and palm trees in an eerie light. Lightning flashes in the distance, illuminating the scene in brief, stark bursts. Heavy clouds churn ominously, threatening to unleash their fury at any moment.

Chapter 2

Enter the platinum blonde bombshell, a vision of Old Hollywood in the flesh. With her overcoat draped on her shoulders and a scarf knotted around her rolled-up hair, she exudes an air of mystery and intrigue. Big Italian sunglasses shield her eyes from any potential prying gazes, adding to her aura of incognito glamour.

As she peels off her shades, revealing green eyes that sparkle with mischief, Bettie can't help but be captivated by the woman before her. With her Jayne Mansfield-style makeup and sassy demeanor, she projects confidence and charm that is impossible to ignore. She's a pulchritudinous force of nature, a reminder of a time when style reigned supreme and beauty knew no bounds.

"Jayne! You scared the life out of me!" Bettie says with a nervous laugh.

Jayne is breathless. "Honey, I just had the life scared out of me. You would not believe the storm out there!"

For a moment, Bettie is transfixed, caught in the gravitational pull of this magnetic woman— her mentor and her friend in this crazy biz. But then, with a flick of her own Bettie Page-inspired locks, she remembers her purpose and her place.

Tonight, they are both performers in a grand spectacle, each bringing their own brand of magic to the stage.

Now Bettie notices the slight, almost imperceptible signs of dishevelment—Jayne's clothes are windswept and glistening with raindrops. But these are no ordinary raindrops—they're *sizzling*.

"What the fuck?" Bettie asks, pointing to Jayne's sleeve.

"What?!" the blonde cries, throwing off her coat. "A bug? What?"

Bettie peers down at the crumpled coat on the threadbare carpet. It's damp, but there's nothing out of the ordinary. She shrugs. "Nothing." Bettie looks around. "I wonder where Irma and Paul are?"

"Are we the first ones here?" Jayne asks. "That's weird. It figures no one's here to witness our early arrival."

"Gatekeeper's here," Bettie says. She eyes the side door. "Why didn't you come in the front?"

Jayne checks her lipstick in the mirror. "The front door is for commoners." Then she laughs. "Just kidding! I parked in the back. My Caddie's too cool for street parking."

One of the perks of working at The Fetish Factory is the company cars. After one year of steady employment, a featured performer is allowed the use of one of the vintage vehicles in the company's fleet. Paul and Irma Wacl's whole life was bringing erstwhile élan back into everyday lives—when they weren't running the more salacious side of their business, they were participating in vintage car shows, selling wares at rockabilly conventions, and sending out real-live singing telegrams via Old Hollywood impersonators. Bettie had dated their Frank Sinatra for a few months, but it didn't work out.

Jayne is now bustling through the room, energetic and pumped up. She walks to the lockers. The main dancers' names mark their spots with Sharpie written on masking tape: BETTIE, JAYNE, ROSIE, TRISTAN, and one with a previous name erased to an indistinct smear. Suddenly, the bible thumper's words echo in Bettie's memory… *Four angels.*

"Figures it's raining," Bettie boohoos, "I hope that won't affect attendance."

"Freak storm, I guess. Don't worry, hon. Nothing's gonna stop tonight's festivities. I am feeling s-e-x-y, sexy!" Jayne takes her trench from the floor and puts it in her locker. She pulls out a vintage 1970s Polaroid camera and points it playfully at her colleague. "Ready for your close-up?"

"Yes, Ms. De Mille!" Bettie strikes a pose, and Jayne snaps a pic. Bettie's head tilts with realization. "We've got The Flasher tonight, don't we?"

"Yep," Jayne affirms, giggling.

Beyond the dirty, neglected, wavy cylinder glass windowpanes, the world outside is a canvas of chaos. Weird, colorful clouds swirl and culminate in a swirl of hues that defy nature's usual palette. Odd flashes of light pierce through the darkness, illuminating the sky with an otherworldly glow, while roaring thunderclaps reverberate through the air like the rumble of distant drums. The gale gathering outside is no ordinary tempest. It is a portent of things to come, a harbinger of events that will shake their world to its core.

But inside the warm, intimate confines of the dressing room, Bettie and Jayne are only peripherally aware of the bizarre changes unfolding outside. They remain cocooned in their own little bubble of anticipation, oblivious to the forces gathering beyond the confines of their dressing room. Their focus is singular, their minds consumed with primping and preparing for the evening ahead. With each stroke of mascara and each spritz of perfume, they steel themselves for their performances—a blend of burlesque comedy and bump-and-grind—their hearts racing. They live for the applause. And the tips.

As Bettie fiddles with her wig, her frustration evident in the furrow of her brow, she can't help but wonder where The Richard, Fetish Factory's resident stylist extraordinaire, has disappeared to. With a sigh, she paraphrases a classic Jayne Mansfield comedy, "The boy can't help it..."

But before she can finish her thought, the door swings open with a flourish and in strides The Richard, a vision of flamboyance and flair. "But am I not worth the wait?!" he declares, his entrance commanding attention like a rock star taking the stage.

Jayne coos in admiration, "You look faaaabulous, dah-ling!" and blows an air kiss in his direction.

His response is characteristically confident. "Tell me something I don't know, honey," he retorts, punctuating his words with a sexy growl.

Bettie, ever the astute observer, appraises him with a critical eye. "Let me guess... tonight you're the love child of Sally Bowles and Ricky Renée with a twist of The Emcee."

The Richard's smile widens, a nod to Bettie's keen eye for fashion. He spreads his arms theatrically, turning to give them a full view of his ultra-glam ensemble, complete with corset and black leather pants. With a flourish, he smooths his long, dark brown hair, a gesture that speaks to his impeccable attention to detail. "Nothing gets by you!"

"Well, I've seen *Cabaret*, like, fifty times," Bettie retorts with a grin.

But before the banter can continue, Jayne interjects, reminding them of their impending performance. "Okay, so not to break up the duet here... but we've gotta get pretty."

The Richard's enthusiasm is palpable. "That's music to my ears!" he exclaims, eager to get his hands on Jayne's glorious locks.

With swift and practiced hands, The Richard works his magic, styling Jayne's hair into the classic Mansfield mane with speed and skill that borders on miraculous.

While the stylist attends to Jayne's coiffure, Bettie occupies herself at the nearby table, her focus on refining the punchlines for this evening's set. Pen and paper in hand, she's been honing her risqué "ventriloquist" routine in collaboration with Gatekeeper. But it lacks that extra kick. A fleeting wish crosses her mind—if only her wooden counterpart bore a closer resemblance to Fats from the 1978 cinematic mindfuck, *Magic.* Such a subtle homage might be lost on The Fetish Factory's patrons, however. Nonetheless, Victor, her existing sidekick, possesses his own charm; his vintage wooden frame, wide-eyed innocence, and rosy-cheeked visage serve as a stark, comedic contrast to the spicy banter he's known for.

Her hand races across the paper as if possessed, her creativity sparking into a frenzy of flippancy. The goal is clear: straddle the fine line between humor and scandal, eliciting from the crowd both ripples of laughter and flushed cheeks. Lines of dialogue take shape under the fervent dance of her pen, vivid proof of her brainstorming.

"Victor, you incorrigible little rascal," she scripts with a smirk, "caught red-handed again, weren't we?" She can almost hear the mixture of gasps and guffaws that will fill the room when she debuts their wicked exchange.

Lost in her writing, Bettie is awash with anticipatory zeal. It's the essence of her passion—the electric surge of live entertainment, the intoxicating rush from the dare of controversy. Some might scorn her performance as tasteless, but such opinions hold no weight for her. She is, after all, the embodiment of burlesque's bold spirit, where provocation is not just welcomed, but celebrated.

As the strains of swing music fill the air, mingling with the scent of industrial-strength hairspray and exotic perfume, Bettie settles into her element, no longer feeling unsettled in the old house. Laughter and chatter fill the air, and a palpable sense of camaraderie and excitement builds.

The connecting door from the office opens, and Irma pokes her head in. "There you are!"

Their imposing boss is dressed in her daily head-to-toe black, her silver-gray streaks blended to perfection with her darker strands to frame her mature, strikingly beautiful but no-nonsense countenance.

"What do you mean?" Bettie protests. "We were the first ones here."

"Oh, were you now?" Irma counters, one perfectly penciled brow cocked. "Come on, it's time to go over tonight's schedule."

Chapter 3

The Fetish Factory's pre-performance powwow unfolds like a scene from a quirky indie film, with the proprietors, Paul and Irma, taking center stage as the retro-square maestros of the evening's festivities. Bettie can't help but admire their juxtaposition: a pair of middle-aged beatniks, all insouciant vibes and brown European cigarillos, but with a business sense sharper than the creases on Paul's black beret. And were they husband and wife, or brother and sister? They shared the same last name, but they kept their relationship mum. Bettie thought they secretly enjoyed the titillation of mystery and speculation.

Rosie and the newest hire, Marilyn, are already on the longest couch, with room left for Bettie and Jayne, who sit side-by-side. Bettie wonders just how early everyone else was and why there was no sign of them when she herself arrived. She makes a mental note to ask Gatekeeper about that.

As Paul adjusts the dimmer switch, casting the room in a moody haze, Bettie's gaze drifts to the portable black and white tube TV in the corner. It plays a medley of old stag films and vintage commercials, a nostalgic trip down memory lane that will soon be projected onto the wall by the bar. It's all part of the experience their customers pay for. The atomic-age coffee table, clean and sleek just moments before, is now a mishmash of drinks, beer bottles, and half-eaten pink frosted donuts—a mess of retro excess.

"Weird weather out there," Irma comments, lighting a cig and taking a long drag.

Her mention of the unexpected rain draws nods from the dancers, each lost in their own world.

Bettie is a vision of vintage vixen bewitchery, boasting a bullet bra, garter belt, and sheer black stockings beneath a silky leopard-print robe. She flips through a movie trivia book, stealing glances at Irma and Paul between pages—she's eager for the meeting to begin and end so she can get to work.

Jayne's blonde waves cascade around her shoulders, framing her heart-shaped face. She's almost stage-ready in her favorite shimmering gold lamé wiggle dress that leaves little to the imagination. With her Polaroid camera in hand, she's the epitome of Old Hollywood glamour, ready to capture the night's moments in all their instant-print glory.

Rosie, the fiery redhead (thanks to a bottle), channels the iconic '40s riveter pinup girl with her crimson bandana and high-waisted denim short-

shorts. On her feet are roller skates. She's staring into space, chewing gum.

Marilyn—making her debut tonight—oozes sex kitten allure in her cheongsam dress with the classic frog collar but with a strategically placed cutout to reveal the full swell of her decolletage. At her tiny waist is a tight black cinch belt with corset lacing. Her makeup is super-exaggerated to enhance a sexy slant on her eyes, and her red lips are perfectly pouty. With a smartphone in hand, she's a modern-day Marilyn Monroe.

Irma takes another drag. "Ladies. Listen up. The rain may be a bitch, but it's not gonna soak our parade. You've all got full dance cards tonight, no cancellations." She reaches for her drink—scotch, on the rocks. The perfectly square, oversized cubes clink. "I'll let you all tell Marilyn here the rules. Since she's new, I won't spank her. Not *yet*, anyway."

Paul sits, stoic. Unreadable.

Rosie taps Marilyn's phone. "No tech, sweetie. Like Irma says. The phone, anything modern you've got—I'm talking pocket change, too… anything pre-1980—it's put in your locker the minute you get here, and not so much as thought of until closing time. Our customers pay a lot for their play days, and we don't disappoint."

Marilyn raises her eyebrows and nods, chastened. "Sorry," she mouths soundlessly.

Jayne adds, "I've been here the longest. Bettie's next. Then Rosie. You're low-man on the totem pole. We'll cut you some slack, but not much. Remember, these guys walk into The Fetish Factory with their fantasies already set. They don't want to hear words like google, selfie, or meme… none of that. When you're here, it's dictionary, Polaroid picture, and the funny papers. Got it?"

Marilyn puts her phone face down on the table and folds her hands neatly in front of her, as if in class.

"Okay, ladies," Irma goes on. Thunder cracks, as if interrupting her. "They say it never rains in Southern California. I'd like to know who this 'they' is and kick'em in the teeth. But the show must go on. Right?" She turns to the youngest girl. "Marilyn, we're glad to have you here. Welcome. Sorry you've got to hit the ground running, but I know you're a smart cookie. You'll catch on quick."

The new dancer smiles shyly. "Thanks. So, I'm wondering… why's tonight so special?"

Irma takes a manly slug of her quickly dwindling drink. "I guess you could say it's our showcase. Most nights, we don't let the clients in. In fact, this is just a pop-up shop. Next time we have a special, we'll be somewhere else. Untraceable. Unattainable. In demand. Usually, we take photos, we make 8mm movies to order. A little phone fun. All sex, all the time."

Marilyn nods again but looks nervous and uncertain.

"But as Paul and I told you when we hired you, no actual sex. This ain't a brothel. You got that? Not only are you not expected to get too friendly with the customers, you're not *allowed* to. No hanky-panky."

"No hanky-panky," Paul affirms, his voice flat.

"No matter how nice they are," Jayne chimes in. "No dating the clients. We sell fantasies, not ourselves. Right, Betts?"

Bettie turns her attention to the night ahead. "Who's on the docket tonight, Paulie?" She nods toward Jayne's camera. "I can guess at least one."

Paul perks up a bit as he consults his notes. "We've got The Flasher, you're right. And Lipstick, Footman, and Whipping Boy. Plus a little crowd for the stage show. You all got your acts down-pat?"

"Been rehearsing like a motherfucker," Bettie says.

Irma scowls. "Language! Naughty, not nasty."

"Right. Sorry." Ever since Bettie had learned that intelligent people tend to curse more than the rest of the human herd, she'd incorporated plenty of colorful language into her everyday discourse. Most men loved it. But The Fetish Factory catered to a different crowd—one that thrived on double entendres, batting lashes, and blushing cheeks.

"Marilyn, sweetie," Irma continued, "it's also important that we make them believe everything is their idea. Like what Henry Ford said, 'If I had asked people what they wanted, they would have said: faster horses.' You know?"

Marilyn blinks, wide-eyed. "Who's Henry Ford?"

"Cliff Robertson," Bettie replies, pointing to her cinematic history book.

Chapter 4

Rosie pops her gum loudly. It sounds like a gunshot. Paul, who's been sweating beneath his black turtleneck, winces in pain. The air in the room grows dense, suffocating, as the stalwart co-leader of The Fetish Factory struggles to maintain his composure. With each passing moment, the sound of the rainfall outside intensifies, its relentless drumming echoing through the vermin-infested walls of the old Queen Anne house.

But it's not just the rain that's amiss. The mundane sounds of the room take on a sinister edge, amplifying to an unbearable cacophony. The turning pages of Bettie's book scrape against his nerves like sandpaper, each rasp sending shivers down his spine. Jayne's fingernails, tapping rhythmically on the tabletop, reverberate through the room like the strikes of a sledgehammer, each impact sending shockwaves of dread through him. Despite his best efforts to conceal it, Paul winces in pain, a silent scream trapped behind gritted teeth.

No one notices his covert discomfort, too consumed by their own preparations for the night ahead. The squall rages on outside, its fury matched only by the growing unease that permeates the room.

Paul's patience frays as he glances at the clock, its ticking now a torturous metronome in his heightened state of irritation. A craving for solitude gnaws at him with the urgency of a trapped animal yearning for escape. He's teetering on the edge of endurance, the presence of others in his vicinity an almost physical assault on his frayed senses. The thought of being alone becomes his silent mantra, a desperate plea amidst the closeness of shared space.

Finally, the gathering draws to a close. His mind hasn't registered the concluding strategy, though it likely deviates little from the norm. Bettie is set to dance and perform her risqué ventriloquist number; Jayne is ready with her clever card illusions; Rosie will glide on her skates, whimsically mimicking the iconic moves of mime Lorene Yarnell. And Marilyn… what was her act again? This lapse in concentration is uncharacteristic of him, a man known for his meticulous oversight of the establishment, yet the ability to focus eludes him now.

As the dancers file from the room, ready to go about their final preparations, oblivious to the gathering storm within, Paul can't shake the feeling that something is terribly wrong. There's a darkness lurking just beyond the edge of their awareness, a malevolent force that threatens to consume them all. He glances up and studies the five women in the room with him; none of them seems agitated in the least.

It's just me, he thinks. *What the devil is wrong with me?*

* * *

Paul begins to feel better as he strolls through the dimly lit hallways, taking in the ornate decor of the rented mini-mansion. Aged chandeliers cast flickering shadows along the walls, playing tricks on his eyes. He runs a hand along the rich, velvet curtains, feeling the plush fabric between his fingers.

Ascending the rickety staircase, he inches toward the door to the room Bettie will be using after the main show ends. He barely makes a sound as he pushes it open, revealing the jungle-themed sanctuary. Verdant fake foliage drapes over every corner, enveloping a luxurious chaise lounge at the room's heart. The rich palette of deep greens complemented by bold leopard prints transports him to a bygone era of tiki bars and exotic escapades. He and Irma have painstakingly selected each piece, hunting down treasures from Hollywood's golden age estate sales and seizing opportunities from tiki establishments bidding their final farewells.

Down the hall, Jayne's pink paradise awaits, dripping with feathers and gold. A vintage photo booth beckons from the corner, ready to capture debaucherous moments. Paul chuckles, already imagining the silly poses she will strike within its cramped confines. With her innate talent for setting the customers at ease, Jayne shines bright. He and Irma have contemplated bringing Jayne into the partnership eventually, but for the present, her sizzling sexiness keeps her performing as a tantalizing attraction.

Rosie's industrial space intrigues with its edgy, rockabilly chic. Distressed metal and rivets offset the soft, pinup aesthetic. He makes a mental note to assign Footman to her room—the visual of a (temporarily) thwarted toe-loving man unlacing Rosie's roller skates as she taunts him sends a delicious shiver down Paul's spine. He knows what the clients like, and he knows that fulfilling their fantasies and leaving them wanting more will fill the coffers with even more cash.

But it isn't until he reaches Marilyn's quarters that his pride truly spikes. Her room is white-on-white, blonde-on-blonde, with a snowy faux-fur rug on the floor and a cream satin settee with a cameo-shaped mirror behind it. Marilyn's timid nature had initially given him pause, but as he steps inside her room and takes in the delicate lace trimming her curtains and the sweet floral scent that lingers in the air, he can't help but feel that there's more to her than meets the eye. Marilyn will make the perfect foil for Whipping Boy, her coyness a stark contrast to the self-flagellation that the masochistic man is known for. Or maybe, just maybe, there is a dormant dominatrix lurking within, waiting to be awakened by the right touch. Paul feels a thrill of excitement at the thought of discovering Marilyn's true nature. He knows her clients will love her, no matter which path she chooses.

A sly grin stretches across Paul's face as the possibilities whirl through his mind, thankfully sharpening his focus. Tonight will be one for the ages.

Chapter 5

The ladies are putting some finishing touches on their makeup and their costumes.

"So, who are these guys…? Lipstick, The Flasher…?" Marilyn asks, her big blue eyes as winsome and innocent as a child's.

"Just guys," Jayne replies reassuringly. "Don't worry, they've got kinks, but they wouldn't hurt a fly. They go by code names."

Bettie adds, "Like *Reservoir Dogs*."

"Huh?" Marilyn says.

"You know, Mr. Pink… Mr. Brown…"

Jayne rolls her eyes. "Don't mind her. She thinks she's gonna be the next Roger Ebert, minus the Pulitzer and tombstone." She turns her attention back to Marilyn. "This is different. These are code names only for us. They don't know what we call them. We don't know their names. I mean, I guess Irma and Paul do. But one of the major perks of The Fetish Factory is anonymity."

Bettie smiles, hoping to reassure the young woman, who reminds her of a Disney fawn.

"How's it different from Only Fans?" Marilyn asks, still confused but obviously wanting to understand.

"Well," Jayne says, the wheel in her mind clearly turning. "Sure, a guy can perv a lady on a webcam and get her to do whatever, but there's always that element of the modern day. They're looking at a computer or tablet screen on the internet, after all. With us, it's close-up and personal… not too personal, of course!" she titters. "Back in the day, the only way to see Jayne Mansfield or Bettie Page in the flesh was if you went to a film premiere or a Hollywood party.

"Plus, everything is truly vintage—Paul and Irma make sure of that every time we do a pop-up like this, which is once or twice a week at the most. The rest of the time, we're at HQ doing made-to-order photoshoots, handwriting letters to our regulars, or talking to them using telephones from the fifties and sixties—they rent phones from us, too, to make sure they're getting the full turnback experience."

"Not only that," Bettie chimes in, "We look at our customers' fetishes like they used to, back in the day. We keep everything secret. 'Hush, hush, on the QT,'" she adds, quoting one of her favorite flicks, *L.A. Confidential.*

"I want Lipstick," Rosie pipes up.

Marilyn helpfully reaches for a tube from the nearby vanity.

Rosie laughs gently. "No, I mean the dude. He's an easy one. He just likes the girls to put makeup on him. He gets off on that."

"Oh, yes, he does!" Jayne giggles. She turns her attention back to Marilyn. "The Footman likes to watch a private dance. He loves a slow striptease. Not with your clothes, but with your heels and stockings. And, he wears gigantic glasses… all the better to see us with."

"Like Jerry Lewis in *The Nutty Professor*." Bettie mimes giant specs with her hands.

Jayne lights a cigarette. "Anyway, as I was trying to say, Footman's got a foot fetish—"

"—Actually, it's a foot fixation," Rosie interrupts. "A fetish is for an inanimate object."

"Thank you, Dr. Drew," Jayne returns dryly. Then she looks down at Marilyn's feet. "Let's see your tootsies. You got nice toes?"

The young woman shakes her head woefully.

"Hmmm," Jayne muses, a hint of mischief sparkling in her eyes. "Okay: Whipping Boy. His name pretty much tells you his deal. Masochist to the max. Then there's The Flasher—he's all mine." She gestures proudly to the lightweight camera that dangles from its plastic strap around her neck. "We're a regular paparazzi duo. Snapshots all night long, honey."

Marilyn's face crinkles with worry, her usual nervousness now edged with panic. "But, what about the performance… onstage? In front of all those people. I haven't had a chance to practice. I'm thrilled to be part of this, I really am, but it's like I'm being fed to the wolves, don't you think?"

Her voice quivers slightly, underlining her trepidation.

"Don't worry, hon. I got your back. The rest of us can handle the choreographed stuff." Jayne says. "If you can call it choreography. Bettie dances, but the rest of us just do old-school bump-and-grind shit. You know, it's strictly burlesque. Have you seen any videos of Tempest Storm? She doesn't peel anything in the first five minutes. Just teases." She pauses. "If you want, you can be our victim."

"Victim?" Marilyn echoes, saucer-eyed.

A new voice joins the conversation. "I'll whip you, you bad little girl."

Heads turn to see the speaker, and all the heavily lashed eyes in the dressing room see tonight's headliner, none other than the fabulous Tristan, enter the dressing room. Bettie and Jayne can't contain their excitement, letting out a synchronized squeal of "Yay, Tristan!" that fills the room with joyous energy.

Tristan basks in the adulation, a Cheshire grin gracing her flawless face. But there's no time to linger in the spotlight—there's work to be done. With practiced efficiency, she sheds her street clothes, revealing the skimpy costume that is her trademark on the stage. She may be a subcontractor for The Fetish Factory, specializing in the art of the bullwhip, but tonight, she's one of the girls, ready to take her place alongside Bettie, Jayne, and the rest of the eclectic ensemble.

Tristan isn't the only star of the show tonight. Dolly Danger and Panama Red will share the spotlight, two titans of the feather fan dance, channeling the spirit of 1930s icon Sally Rand with every graceful flick of their wrists. Semi-regular Fetish Factory freelance impersonators of Suzie Wong and Josephine Baker will do one dance each. And then there's the female-fronted sixties-style rock band, plus the torch singer, whose sultry melodies will set the stage on fire, figuratively speaking.

Bettie and Jayne, ever the consummate artistes, have studied the classics of vaudville, always ready to keep the audience guessing with a ventriloquist act, card tricks, or even a bit of aerial yoga. And on the rare occasion when they can rent a snake, well, let's just say their tandem python dance is not to be missed. Rosie does a silent striptease down to red-spangled pasties and a G-string on her baby blue suede roller skates, channeling a 1940s WAC, blowing bubbles with her invisible wad of Bazooka gum all the while.

Irma pops into the room. "Almost ready, ladies? We've got a full house. Which ain't sayin' much in this dive, but it pays the bills."

"Amen to that," Jayne says. "God forbid I should have to get a real job."

"Or a real boyfriend," Bettie adds. "Are you still seeing BOB?" As in, battery-operated boyfriend.

Jayne sighs dramatically. "That's rich, coming from you."

"Heyyy! My single status is entirely by choice." Bettie protests.

Jayne turns to Marilyn. "She broke up with her last boyfriend because he didn't want to go to an all-night horror-fest with her."

"It wasn't just any all-night horror-fest," Bettie sputters. "It was giallo and nunsploitation. Big difference!"

Chapter 6

Her compatriots rib her for her encyclopedic knowledge of film trivia, yet for Bettie, her geeky façade serves as armor. It not only guards her vulnerable heart but also keeps her connected to the memories of her mother.

Growing up, Bettie held her mom in high esteem, idolizing her not just as a hardworking, loving single parent but as the once-in-demand pinup model known as Belinda Joy. Her mother's radiant beauty and unwavering confidence were the pillars that inspired Bettie, sowing the early seeds of her own fascination with fashion and the art of performance.

Their weekends were enchanting escapes into cinematography's embrace, where they would rent armloads of DVDs from their corner video store, Flickers of the Past—a last bastion of physical media, barely hanging on. Netflix mail-order video rentals had just started becoming a thing, but tween Bettie was an old soul who loved searching the shelves for both rare and classic gems.

Nestled on their sofa in the suburbs, mom and daughter shared buttery popcorn and the warmth of their giggles, diving deep into their picks. They reveled in Marilyn Monroe's magnetism and

Audrey Hepburn's timeless elegance, idolizing their grace and poise. These iconic women of Hollywood's golden era were not just entertainers to Bettie and Belinda; they were muses.

During those intimate movie marathons, the spark of Bettie's love for performance came to life. She'd watch, utterly captivated by the dramatic flair of the actresses and dancers, dreaming of the day when she'd command the stage with a similar charisma, dazzling crowds with her own unique blend of charm and wit.

Yet, their connection transcended the admiration of screen sirens and style. It was through their shared passion for the cinematic world that the pair found comfort and a deep sense of kinship in trying times. The movies became their refuge, whether they were contending with the turbulent waves of adolescence or dealing with the gaping void left by Bettie's father, who had vanished without a trace when she was only two years old.

Their film collection was eclectic, yet some stood out for their personal resonance. *Gypsy*, inspired by the memoirs of burlesque legend Gypsy Rose Lee, played my Natalie Wood, chronicled the performer's ascent to stardom under her formidable mother's management—a stark contrast to Bettie's own nurturing and open-hearted mom. Belinda taught her daughter to embrace the artistry of pinups and dancers, emphasizing that if a woman pursued such a path out of love, it was nothing but honorable. *Lady of Burlesque*, which catered to Bettie's affinity for suspense and the macabre, starred Barbara Stanwyck in a film noir that unraveled a series of murders in a glamorous cabaret theater. And then there was *I'm No Angel*, with Mae West portraying a burlesque star imbued with her signature sharp jabs and lewd humor. From Mae, Bettie borrowed a spark for her own risqué and comical ventriloquist act.

Bettie's world was upended at the tender age of fifteen by her mother's death—a life-changing event that some never anticipate, while others watch approach like an oncoming train, powerless to stop it. The abrupt passing of Belinda from cancer during Bettie's formative teenage years severed their weekend film rituals like a broken reel. Suddenly alone, grappling with the complexities of growing up and the sting of bereavement, Bettie clung to the solace found in those treasured cinematic moments with her mother, seeking refuge in the beloved films that had cradled their bond.

In the wake of her loss, the courts granted her emancipation, and she stepped into adulthood prematurely, juggling retail and waitressing jobs before finding her rhythm in dance. Her path eventually led her to The Fetish Factory, where she reveled in the creative freedom offered by

Paul and Irma, crafting characters that paid homage to her mother's memory with a blend of sexiness and sass.

Now Bettie was carrying forth her mother's legacy, her fervor for fashion and performing arts more than just pastimes—they were an homage to the woman who had sculpted her very essence. As she navigated the twists and turns of the burlesque scene and the world beyond, Bettie clutched her mother's memory close to her heart, channeling her spirit for courage, invigorated by the enduring love and cinematic passion they had cultivated together.

When she wasn't working, Bettie sought fleeting moments of respite on The New Beverly Theater's sagging screen. Immersed in a diverse filmic tapestry—French New Wave, madcap sixties Italian sex comedies, grindhouse features, exploitation flicks, slashers, and horror classics— she indulged her appetites.

Her film education was anything but ordinary. It was a cinematic odyssey sans classroom walls, where the flicker of an old projector bulb was her overhead light and the mouthwatering aroma of popcorn her educational incentive. Instead of a formal curriculum, she was schooling herself through a marathon of movie masterpieces, one epic story at a time.

In lieu of stuffy lectures, her professors were the wisecracking heroes and villainous masterminds that danced across the silver screen—a charismatic ensemble cast teaching her the art of snappy dialogue and the perfect dramatic pause. Forget the typical pomp of an academic procession… Bettie's graduation march was the iconic theme song of an opening credit roll echoing down the sloping aisle.

Study sessions consisted of back-to-back feature films, and her notes were a collection of ticket stubs, each one a reminder of the plot twist or character arc that had captivated her that day. She scoffed at the mere thought of multiple-choice tests when the real challenge lay in unriddling a director's symbolic use of mise-en-scène or decoding the subtext of a foreign film without subtitles.

Homework? That was a rigorous regimen of freeze-frames and rewinds as she dissected the anatomy of a chase sequence or the nuances of a love scene until the VHS tape whimpered for mercy. She wasn't just watching; she was engaging in an interactive tutorial where every rewind was a lesson learned and every fast forward a glimpse into storytelling efficiencies.

Her film studies were an enchanted blend of pop quizzes populated by aliens and time-travelers, and her electives were in the form of binge-watching noir by the glow of a solitary lamp. It was a wonderfully rogue educational path, garnished with more plot twists and climaxes than the most imaginative professor could ever concoct.

Indeed, it was an education of the most critically acclaimed sort—no diploma required, just an insatiable love for the movies and an endless supply of sugary and salty snacks. Bettie was a summa cum laude graduate of the silver screen. And her capstone project was living life with the flair and resolve of a leading lady in the grand movie of existence.

Chapter 7

Irma acts as the bawdy emcee. She tells jokes as old as Wild Bill's buckskin condom, but with the sass and sex only a broad like her can sell. The mermaid hem of her floor-length, skintight silver gown glimmers under the spotlight, accentuating every curve as she sashays across the stage. In her hand, a painted fan flirts with the air, an extension of her teasing persona, while her arms disappear into long, elbow-length gloves, the epitome of élan. Behind her, a small jazz trio plays, their presence nearly swallowed by the shadows at the back of the stage, yet their laid-back tunes form the heartbeat of the room.

"Welcome, fellas. Welcome to The Fetish Factory. We've got a heck of a show for you gentlemen tonight. Now, our first peeler's a real peach. Bettie's her name. Gorgeous. Sexy. Sweet." She fans herself and pulls a face. "She ain't perfect, though. I don't want to say she's a drunk, but just last week, she was put in front of a judge. The judge says, 'You've been brought here for drinking.' Bettie here says, 'Okay, let's get started!'"

The crowd applauds, then starts whistling when they see Bettie.

She struts onto the stage, her every step oozing a sensual rhythm that's in sync with the seductive tunes from the shadows. Her flirty feathered fans flutter, teasing the audience with glimpses of her curvaceous figure. Beside her, new girl Marilyn stumbles through her steps, a clumsy yet endearing contrast to the star's seasoned grace. With a playful swat, Bettie unties the knot of Marilyn's cheongsam top, revealing a pair of pasties that are mere dots on her bounteous bosom.

Holding a fan in front of Marilyn, Bettie creates an air of anticipation, the audience's attention glued to the makeshift barrier. With a glint in her eyes, Bettie lets out an exaggerated "Ooops!" as the fan slips from her grip, offering a tantalizing flash of Marilyn's breasts. The young girl, theatrically taken aback, turns around in mock embarrassment, her cheeks flushed a deep petal pink. As the applause and catcalls echo through the room, she exits the stage, taking the fans with her, leaving Bettie to bask in the spotlight.

Bettie sweeps across the stage, her black wig shimmering under the stage lights, a stark contrast to the paleness of her skin. The air is thick with smoke and anticipation. She grabs an old wooden chair from the back, its legs scraping against the floor in a low, satisfying rumble. Center stage, she plants it with a thud that demands attention.

From a nearby box stamped with faded circus letters, she retrieves an object swaddled in red velvet. She unfolds the cloth with care, revealing a ventriloquist's dummy, its painted eyes reflecting the crowd's hungry gaze. She takes a seat, resting the doll in her lap.

Bettie smiles sweetly, her eyes sparkling scampishly as she addresses the captivated crowd. "Hello, gentlemen. I'm Bettie," she purrs, her voice dripping with sarcasm, "and this is my dummy, Victor."

She pauses for a beat, her grip tightening on the inner mechanism. The room is silent, the anticipation palpable. Then, a deep, indignant voice fills the air, "Victoria, *dummy!*"

Bettie can't help but chuckle. Perfect, she thinks. Gatekeeper is hidden behind the speakers stacked up on the far right of the stage. He's got the script written down, every line and cue meticulously noted. She can't deviate from it, not even a little. But *this*, this is so much better than the cassette tape she used to use for Victor's lines.

She remembers that one disastrous night when the player had eaten the tape, the thin magnetic ribbon spilling out like the guts of a mechanical beast. But she had played it off, incorporated it into the act, and no one had been the wiser. Naturally, the audience was too busy gawking at her dazzling, derriere-baring costume and flawless moves to notice the technical snafu. But hey, that's the thrill, right? It's like walking a tightrope without a net, except the net is her talent and professionalism.

She forges ahead. "Victoria? What are you talking about? You are clearly male. See, this is what's wrong with our relationship. It's the different sex thing. Most ventriloquist-dummy partnerships are same-sex. Have you noticed? And they're not about sex at all."

"Of course I've noticed, sweetheart," Victor leers with his hinged grin.

"You see? You called me 'sweetheart.' A sex vibe has crept in."

"Ya think?"

The men in the audience titter with laughter, their faces glowing in the stage lights as they guffaw at the provocative back-and-forth between Bettie and her wooden counterpart. Victor, dressed to the nines in a vintage black tie infant's outfit, complete with a tiny top hat, is the perfect foil to Bettie's soft, curvaceous form. She loves the thrill of the stage, the way she can make the audience eat out of the palm of her hand with just a wink or a well-timed joke.

"Just what kind of a relationship are a female ventriloquist and a male dummy going to have? We can't just be good old buddies, can we?" she asks, batting her lashes.

"A friend on the knee is a friend indeed."

"Besides, your voice is all wrong."

"What's wrong with my voice?"

"Well, you see, with a same-sex team, the ventriloquist, me, doesn't need to change her voice to sound like a girl. When you talk, Victor, my throat is scratchy all night."

"Oh, I don't think your sore throat has anything to do with me, sweetheart!"

The crowd erupts in a cacophony of whoops and whistles, a flurry of dollar bills spinning through the air like miniature paper airplanes, landing with a soft rustle on the stage. Bettie's eyes sparkle with delight, her heart pounding in rhythm with the lively music as she basks in the glow of approval.

Bettie straightens her posture to an exaggerated degree, displaying a theatrical sense of indignation. "Well, I never! If you're not careful, I'll turn you into kindling!"

"I've already got wood, if you know what I mean…"

A chorus of "Oohs" rises from the audience.

Victor's mouth clacks open. "Geez, Bettie, this crowd's stiffer than my joints!"

The guys laugh, but Bettie shoots her partner a mock glare that softens into an amused smirk. "Behave yourself," she scolds him as she adjusts his tiny bow tie. "We've got company."

Victor turns to the crowd, his painted head swiveling with mechanical precision. "Ah, forgive me, folks. It's not every day I get to see such a beautiful bunch of sinners."

Bettie leans in closer to the puppet. "Tell me, Vic," she purrs, "ever been to a burlesque show before?"

Victor's huge, painted eyes seem to widen just a fraction. "Only when you leave your closet door open."

More laughter.

She gives him a playful tap on the nose. "Cheeky," Bettie retorts with a twinkle in her eye.

Victor straightens up as if bracing for his next line. "I'm just happy to be out of that box. It was like being at my own funeral—too quiet and not enough booze."

Bettie beams as chuckles and snorts rise from the tables scattered around the dimly lit room. The warmth of the spotlight feels like summer sunshine on her face but she's aware of the crashing downpour outside and her mind wanders to the convertible parked outside... even with the cover, it's bound to leak.

Victor looks up at her with his glassy stare. "Say, what do you call an undead burlesque dancer?"

Bettie raises an eyebrow—this isn't part of the script—but plays along. "I don't know, Vic. What?"

"A zombabe!" He cackles at his own joke as Bettie rolls her eyes showily. *Good one, Gatekeeper,* she thinks.

The audience joins in the dummy's laughter, their amusement hanging in the air along with their cigar smoke.

Bettie, her indignation a mere façade, rises to her full height and seizes Victor's arm, gently shaking him as if he were a disobedient child. "Back in the box you go, you naughty, naughty little man!" she declares, her voice ringing out above the lively music and the crowd's enthusiasm.

With a deft flick of her wrist, she turns the puppet's face to the crowd, using her concealed hand to shrug his little shoulders in a gesture of contrition. *Well, now I've done it!* the dummy seems to be thinking, and the men in the audience respond with a hearty chorus of wolf whistles and applause.

"You tell him!" Lipstick shouts.

"I'm a bad boy too," Whipping Boy calls out, his words only serving to fuel the raucous energy as Bettie concludes her sassy show.

She carefully places the vintage dummy back into its designated box, the echoes of applause and whistles from the enamored crowd reverberating in her ears. She gracefully exits the stage with a confident stride, her lips curling into a coy, sly smile that hints at the fun-loving personality hidden beneath her glamorous Bettie Page façade.

Irma, ever the flamboyant mistress of ceremonies, takes the stage once more with her signature panache and charisma, commanding the attention of everyone in the room.

"Let's give it up one more time for our stunning, seductive dancers!" she declares, her voice brimming with excitement and a touch of dramatic flair. "And folks, the night is far from over! We've got some extra special, extraordinary, exemplary acts lined up for you that you simply can't afford to miss!"

Tristan, Panama Red, and Dolly Danger glide into the spotlight, their bodies radiating an aura of mystery and seduction. With a grace that can only be honed through years of practice, they begin their elaborate fan dances, the feathers fluttering in time with the sultry strains of classic burlesque music. An instrumental medley of "Fever," "I Put a Spell on You," and "The Lady Is a Tramp" dances on air in accompaniment to the ladies' hypnotic blend of sensuality and skill, holding the men in the audience spellbound.

Their cheers and catcalls echo through the room, punctuating the space like exclamation marks in a racy novel.

Backstage, Bettie surveys the audience, her eyes lingering on the familiar faces that never seem to miss a show. There's Lipstick, his eyes gleaming with a wily expression, his hair slicked back in the style of a 1930s movie idol. Footman is there too, looking dapper in his trademark bowtie and suspenders, his glasses magnifying his already bulging eyes. Whipping Boy, resplendent in his loud, garish Hawaiian-print shirt, brandishes his riding crop with a flourish, his jolly laughter ringing out above the music. And, of course, there's The Flasher, the mustachioed man who wears nothing but tighty-whities under his long trench coat.

Tristan, Red, and Dolly finish their dance, then stand in a row, taking a bow in unison.

Irma claims the spotlight, shooing the girls away with her hand fan. "Now, we have the scintillating, seductive, and stylish Jayne for you," she announces into her mic, her voice locked and loaded with anticipation as she swans across the small stage.

Jayne emerges from behind the Marshall stacks, a vision in skintight gold latex and a fascinator hat perched jauntily atop her head. Irma shoots her a pointed look before launching into a playful anecdote. "As you can see, she has beautiful golden locks. It's natural, too. Yeah, she's your classic dumb blonde. I was with Jayne here when she went to get her new driver's license last week. She took one look at it and started wailing. I said, 'Honey, what's wrong?' Jayne turns to me and says, 'Look—I got an F in sex!'"

The audience erupts into mirth, Jayne joining in with a good-natured wink. Irma flounces offstage and Jayne takes over, her movements smooth and fluid. With a flirtatious flick of her leg, she produces a deck of cards from her thigh garter, holding them aloft for all to see before tucking them into her cleavage with a mischievous look.

"In my bosom here, I have an ordinary deck of playing cards," she declares, leaning forward to give the men an eyeful.

The audience responds with enthusiastic handclapping, their appreciation for Jayne's charms evident in their noisy cheers and whistles.

"You know, I don't think our special guests can *reeeeeaaaalllly* see these cards." Her eyes sweep over the reserved area that's especially set aside for the special four men who'll get private shows later on. Jayne steps to the edge of the stage and leans over, closer.

Her frisky gaze sweeps across the eager faces in the audience, her lips curling into a cupid's bow. "May I have a volunteer, please?" she calls out, her voice carrying a hint of theatrical panache.

Instantly, hands shoot up into the air, a chorus of voices clamoring for the performer's attention as they vie to be selected for the coveted role. But Jayne, the unpredictable show-woman that she is, bypasses the eager volunteers and instead singles out the one who hadn't raised his hand—a well-dressed, tall, thin man with long, straight, dark hair. His smile is shy, his eyes sparkling with anticipation as he steps forward to join Jayne on stage.

"So... what do you want me to do?" he asks, his voice marked with nervous excitement.

"Pick a card, any card," Jayne replies, her tone inviting as she gestures toward the deck nestled against her breasts.

The volunteer hesitates for a moment, his fingers hovering uncertainly over the cards. But Jayne's reassuring smile and the encouraging murmurs of the audience embolden him, and with a decisive motion, he plucks the Queen of Hearts from the well-worn deck.

"Now," Jayne says, "Don't show me your card. You'll spoil the surprise. But do show them." She gestures to the patrons.

Holding it up for all to see, he displays the card to his fellow audience members before carefully returning it to its rightful place amidst the other cards in the deck.

"Thank you," Jayne says with honey warmth, her appreciation evident as she gestures for the volunteer to return to his seat. "You're a prince among men."

As the man makes his way back to the audience, a ripple of applause follows in his wake, his brief moment in the spotlight adding an extra touch of excitement to the evening's festivities.

Jayne weaves her enchantment with the effortless finesse only years of dedication could bestow, and Bettie, nestled in the shadows just offstage, feels a familiar affection swell within her. The spellbinding dance of burlesque, with its potent blend of mystery and provocation, and her sisterhood with her colleagues, holds her heart in a way nothing else can.

Jayne shuffles the cards and "accidentally on purpose" fumbles and they fly into the air in fifty-two different directions. "Oh, no. Look what I've done," she exclaims, all feminine and helpless. "Butterfingers!" She looks over her shoulder to the backstage area. "New girl! Oh Marilyn, where are you? I need help picking up these cards."

Marilyn hesitates for a brief moment, then joins Jayne on the stage. The scene transforms into a playful hunt, both ladies on their hands and knees, a comedic tableau against the bawdy backdrop. Bills flutter down like confetti, but the women pay them no mind. Their focus is singular—to retrieve every last card.

Bettie watches, amusement lighting her eyes as the men continue to shower the stage with currency, their eagerness undiminished by the performers' disregard for the tips.

Suddenly, Jayne notices something in Marilyn's cleavage. Her eyes grow wide. "What's that, Marilyn?"

Marilyn shrugs, all wide-eyed innocence.

"Stand up," Jayne says, rising to her own high-heeled feet. "Lemme see. Looks like you're smuggling something there… and it ain't cantaloupes."

Jayne, her curiosity pretentiously piqued, leans in towards Marilyn, her fingers deftly slipping into the sequined bra-top. With a flourish, she retrieves the Queen of Hearts, the missing card from their earlier trick. The card glints under the stage lights as she holds it high, a triumphant smile playing on her plump, pink lips.

The audience erupts into a cacophony of applause and whistles, and the girls make their exit, leaving the stage to their boss.

Irma struts out, her vintage silver microphone in hand, its long black cord trailing. The lights dance across her ample, zaftig figure, casting shadows and highlights that only serve to enhance her dramatic presence. Bettie notices the way her silver gown appears to liquefy into streams of molten metal beneath the intense illumination. The stage lights hail from a bygone era, employing antiquated, scorching bulbs. Gleaming chrome 1950s Patt23 lights adorn the space, casting a hard light on one side of the mature woman's face.

"You might have noticed we have a new young lady here on stage," she says to the men. "You see, I had to fire somebody. It wasn't easy, but that girl was dense as a doorknob and she had an attitude to boot. When I told her I'd slept with a Brazilian, she said, 'Oh my god! You hussy! How many is a Brazilian?'"

Chapter 8

Irma dominates the stage, her presence both magnetic and commanding, while Paul devotes himself to the seamless behind-the-scenes operation of the show.

The diligent proprietor maneuvers a garment rack filled with an array of costumes into the dressing area, providing the performers with a diverse wardrobe choice for their upcoming acts. Although he had convinced himself of his improving condition, a profound weariness engulfs him the moment he sinks into the vanity chair. It's an overwhelming sensation that drags him into a murky sea of mud. A peculiar craving gnaws at him—a hunger for meat, a yearning that is utterly foreign to his long-standing vegetarian values. Terror twists within him, for such cravings have no place in his reality since he eschewed meat over three decades ago.

Chewed... meat... something in his mind whispers.

With a heavy sigh, Paul gazes into the mirror, the lightbulbs framing his image and casting an ethereal glow around him. But as he searches his own face, he feels a creeping sense of unease tearing at the edges of his consciousness. It's as if he's staring into the eyes of a stranger, a feeling of disconnection settling over him like a shroud.

The reflection in the mirror holds Paul's gaze, its eyes clouded with confusion. Why had he stumbled into the girls' dressing room? The thought seemed to dance just out of reach, taunting him with its elusiveness. The scent of powder and perfume fills the air, mingling with a faint, metallic tang that he can't quite place.

His head spins, a carousel of fragmented memories and sensations whirling inside his skull. The sound of laughter and the click of high heels echo from beyond the door, yet here he sits, ensnared in a silent struggle to piece together his own narrative.

Paul lifts a hand to his forehead, feeling the sweat that has begun to bead along his hairline. He squints at the array of cosmetics scattered across the vanity, their bright colors a stark contrast to the gray pallor of his skin.

A sequined dress hung on the wardrobe door catches his eye—sparkling crimson, it seems to pulse with a life of its own. Has he brought it here for one of the performers? The question lingers unanswered as another wave of dizziness sweeps over him.

He attempts to stand but falters, clutching at the edge of the vanity for support. The bulbs around the mirror flicker momentarily, casting erratic shadows across his face.

"Get it together, daddy-o," he mutters under his breath, a mantra more than an assurance. He glances once more into the mirror, trying to recognize himself in the man who looks back at him—a man now marked by an inexplicable hunger and a disquieting sense of alienation from his own flesh and blood.

Blinking away the disorientation, Paul's heart is a hamster on a wheel as his eyes flicker, momentarily engulfed in an unsettling whiteness that seems to swallow his very soul. The sensation passes as quickly as it came, leaving him trembling and bewildered. What's happening to him? He hasn't felt right since he arrived earlier this evening, a nagging sense of foreboding lurking just beneath the surface of his consciousness.

Suddenly, a grating sound pierces the silence, amplified in Paul's head like a discordant punk rock song. He winces, his senses on high alert as he detects the faint sound of someone attempting to open the window in the girls' dressing room. With a scowl, Paul approaches the casement, his pulse quickening with each step.

But before he can investigate further, movement catches his eye—a massive, mangy rat scuttling across the floor, its red eyes gleaming in the muted light. Paul recoils in disgust, wiping the cold sweat from his upper lip as he hurries back into the office, the need for a moment of relief overwhelming him.

Unbeknownst to Paul, a mysterious figure lurks outside, concealed in the shadows cast by the foliage. Clad in dark-wash jeans and a hoodie, shielded from the rain with a black umbrella, the figure paces anxiously, its gaze fixed on the closed front door. There's a palpable tension in the air, a sense of anticipation and agitation. If Paul had looked out the window, he might have glimpsed the figure, but for now, he remains unaware of the danger lurking just beyond the threshold.

* * *

The office offers a thin veil of solitude, the thumping bass and the cheers from the crowd beyond its walls a constant reminder of the show he is missing. Paul leans back in his chair, allowing the leather to embrace his weary form. He knows his place is out there, pressing flesh with the patrons, ensuring their glasses remain full and their pockets empty. These men, clad in their crisp suits and slick smiles, are the foundation upon which The Fetish Factory thrives.

But tonight, Paul's usual affability and energy are mere phantoms. His head pounds with an intensity that seems to keep time with the music, each beat a hammer to the cranium. A sickness clings to him, subtle yet persistent, sapping what little strength he has left.

He stands and paces the small space, passing by framed photos of past shows that adorn the walls. The images depict scenes of vibrant performances and lively crowds—in utter contrast to the pallor of his own reflection that haunts him from the darkened windowpane.

A few more minutes, he thinks. Just a few more to gather himself.

With hands that tremble ever so slightly, Paul opens the bottom drawer of his desk and retrieves a bottle of gin—his indulgence for nights when the weight of management bears down too heavily on his shoulders. And, if he's being honest, nights when things are going well. He uncaps the bottle and pours a generous amount into a glass, foregoing ice or any pretense of savoring the drink. The clear liquid catches the light as he swirls it in the glass, a momentary distraction from the discomfort that grips him.

A long gulp burns its way down Paul's throat, leaving behind a trail of warmth that seems to seep into his very bones. He exhales deeply, feeling the alcohol begin to dull the sharper edges of his malaise. Another sip follows as Paul closes his eyes and lets the sounds of Irma's voice waft through the door—a siren's call beckoning him back to life outside this room.

He can almost see her on stage now: captivating the audience with her unparalleled grace, fiery gaze, and howler jokes. He takes another drink, letting the gin do its work. The sensation isn't immediate, but gradually, as if emerging from a fog, Paul begins to feel steadier on his feet. His head still throbs dully in protest, but it no longer feels as if it might split open at any moment.

Another belt for good measure; then he'll rejoin his guests. He promises himself just one more swig—enough gumption in a glass to face whatever awaits him beyond these four walls.

Chapter 9

Irma strides boldly but gracefully. She makes her way close to the edge of the stage.

"Next up, we've got the riveting redhead, Rosie! You may have noticed she likes to skate. Yep, we appreciate a peeler who's in shape. Me, I'm not in shape. Rosie wanted me to enroll in her aerobics class. I told her, 'No. Absolutely not.' Because I tried that once. I twisted, hopped, jumped, stretched, and pulled. And by the time I got those darn leotards on, the class was over!" A rimshot punctuates the joke.

From the wings of the stage, Bettie continues to watch with a mixture of admiration and amusement as Rosie, the vivacious vixen on roller skates, glides onto the spotlighted stage.

Clad in the iconic denim and red polka-dot bandana, and Betty Grable short-shorts, she creates her character to perfection, her easy charm seizing the audience's attention. With practiced ease, Rosie begins her act, her movements fluid as she mimics being trapped in an invisible box, her expression a perfect blend of faux frustration and dogged determination. Each twist and turn of her body is executed with precision, her skates propelling her across the stage with effortless finesse.

But it's Rosie's next move that truly steals the show. With a cheeky smile, she produces a giant, invisible chewing gum bubble, blowing it with exaggerated gusto until it reaches comically oversized proportions. The audience erupts into laughter and applause, their enthusiasm infectious as they eagerly anticipate what comes next.

With a toss of her cerise hair, Rosie allows the gum to pop with a satisfying snap (thanks to the band's drummer), sending flecks of imaginary pink goo flying in all directions. With a mock gasp of surprise, she feigns dismay as the sticky substance lands on her chest, threatening to ruin her costume. But Rosie is nothing if not resourceful. With a coquettish smile, she teasingly removes her top, revealing just enough to tantalize without revealing too much.

The men go wild, their cheers and whistles ringing in her ears as she deftly turns the mishap into a moment of teasing seduction. As a capper, she tosses the top out into the audience, and it lands on Whipping Boy's balding head.

It's a performance that leaves the audience captivated and eager for more, setting the stage for Bettie's own grand finale.

* * *

The storm outside is a relentless beast, its howling winds and pounding rain practically begging for an invitation inside. The old house currently playing dress-up as The Fetish Factory's hideout shudders under the siege, its geriatric timbers groaning louder than a nursing home at bedtime. The lights flicker on and off like a strobe with commitment issues, casting shadows that twist and dance in the corners.

Bettie catches a glimpse of the backstage window sill. Of course, it's wide open—gulping down rainwater and turning the wooden floor into a slip-and-slide. She sighs, then walks over to close it. Sure, the job is a hoot—the dazzle, the winning smiles, the endless sparkle. But sometimes, the pop-up venue selections by Paul and Irma range from sketchy to "Are we filming a murder documentary here?"

Lincoln Heights, while distinctly not Hollywood, boasts its own charm—if one finds broken dreams and misspelled graffiti charming. Bettie can't help but shiver, feeling more goosebumps than sequins and lace. *Mental note to self: Beg someone burly named Gatekeeper to brave the shadowy trek to the car, post-show.*

As the music takes a smoke break, an arresting silence crashes the party. Bettie hears the oh-so-delightful pitter-patter of rats auditioning for a tap-dancing gig in the dark. She shoves aside a cringe and throws a glance towards Victor, who looks decidedly sinister and sentient, thanks to the lightning makeover. Dry throat? Check. Need alcohol? Absolutely.

She saunters to the bar, walls shaking like an architectural twerking competition, her hips keeping beat with the tantrum of the tempest. The lady bartender throws her the kind of nod you'd expect at an undertaker's networking event. Bettie orders her whiskey neat because it's that kind of night and knocks it back like she's the vanquisher of thirsty specters.

One look at the taunting clock—tick-tock, your life's escaping—and it's nearly curtain call for the grand finale. The world could end in a downpour, but Bettie's storm brews from within, ready to claim the stage. The external whirlwind can scream its heart out; it's just background noise to Bettie's own electrical charge.

Chapter 10

Restlessness pulls at Paul's insides as he sinks back into the lumpy sofa, the cacophony of burlesque music from the small three-piece live band still assaulting his senses. Funny, but he'd been reluctantly considering hearing aids last week, and now he had the perception of a newborn elephant. Worse, the drinks he downed did jack to ease his worries.

Desperate for relief, Paul makes his way to the bar tucked discreetly behind the small audience of eager patrons. He sees Bettie leaving and hopes she's not too sloshed to stay on her feet during the finale dance. He adores Bettie like a daughter… or maybe more like a naughty niece, but damn, that girl can sure set'em up and knock'em back.

The bartender, adorned in a corset and with a fascinator perched atop her curls like a crown, beams a smile that could rival the spotlights. Her hands dance a ballet of bottles and shakers, a blur of clinks and pours, and within a span of sixty seconds, several connections are lined up. A server takes the drinks, puts them on a silver platter, and heads to the performance room.

Paul approaches and puts his hands on the bar, steadying himself. "Hey, Barkeep. I feel like a Zombie tonight," he grumbles. His longing for the near-fatal, potent tiki concoction mirrors his thirst for oblivion, a desperate escape from his fretting but fleeting thoughts.

"You got it, sir!" she chirps, her voice a melody amid the cacophony as she pushes a drink toward him. It's a simpler mixture, lacking the intricate layers of a true Zombie, but Paul's not in a position to protest. The warming caress of the booze promises a temporary reprieve from the constant hum of dread that lingers below the surface.

In a corner, Gatekeeper stands like a surly sentinel, his eagle-like gaze sweeping over the patrons with the precision of a lighthouse beam. "Not much of a crowd tonight," he remarks, a subtle hint of disappointment weaving through his words. Paul knows his bouncer loves the opportunity to throw someone out on their ear—that's rare, though. Mostly, Paul and Irma subscribe to 'the customer is always right' philosophy… unless there's disrespect shown to the talent.

Paul nods in agreement, his gaze drifting aimlessly over the dwindling audience. Despite selling out and boasting a full house, only half the expected clientele have shown up, and half of them are leaving early. "Tell me about it. Wives expect their husbands to stay home on rainy nights. At this rate, who's gonna keep Irma and me in imported cigarillos?"

"Smoking is a nasty habit. Someday it'll kill ya," Gatekeeper remarks, crossing his arms and displaying the impressive bulge of his biceps. A testament to clean living, his physique certainly wasn't sculpted from indulging in vices like drinking and smoking.

At least I don't eat meat, Paul thinks. Then, his stomach grumbles with anticipation and his mouth waters. "This rain is what's gonna kill me," he mutters, the weight of his frustration imbuing his words with a sulky undertone.

As Irma introduces another act with her characteristic panache, Paul's head continues to throb in time with the thudding rhythm of the drums and guitars. The lights from the stage flicker and dance before his eyes, exacerbating his growing discomfort. He feels sick, his stomach churning with a queasy unease that he just can't shake. Why does he feel like this? What's wrong with him? The questions swirl through his mind like a maelstrom, leaving him adrift in a sea of mystification.

Paul's gaze drifts to the stage, his thumping headache momentarily forgotten as Kelly, the next act, steps into the spotlight. She's a crooner, her breathy voice capable of weaving a spell over the audience with just a single note. As the Dorothy Dandridge lookalike settles behind her keyboard, a hush falls over the room, the clinking of glasses and murmured conversations fading into silence.

The musician's deft, dark fingers dance across the keys, a ballet of black and white, as she begins to play. The melody is hauntingly beautiful, a ballad that she penned herself, and it weaves its way through the air like a ribbon of smoke. The audience leans forward, their collective breaths held, as they wait for her to sing.

When she does, her voice is a siren's call, a sonata of seduction. She's skimpily dressed, just like the dancers, her curves on full display for the appreciative male audience. It's a necessary evil, a compromise she's willing to make to share her music with the world. And while her ballad is randy, the innuendo and double entendres artfully woven into the lyrics, it's also heartbreakingly beautiful, an ode to the power of love and desire.

As Kelly's song reaches its crescendo, Paul's thoughts drift to Irma, his wife... or sister, nobody knows. And that's how they like it. He loves her, of course, but tonight, he's feeling... restless. He glances over at Bettie, the burlesque queen who's become something akin to family. She's gorgeous, her hourglass figure a throwback to the glamour of old Tinsel Town. But it's her sassy, sarcastic sense of humor that truly sets her apart, her adroit wit and clever quips a constant source of amusement for Paul. If only he were thirty years younger. *If only Bettie were edible.* He wonders what her beautiful blue eyes squishing between his molars would taste like.

As the applause for Kelly's performance fills the room, Paul's thoughts turn even darker. Why is his body plagued by this strange, gnawing hunger? It's like he's slowly... changing, his humanity slipping away like sand through a sieve.

As the night wears on, Paul's resolve begins to falter. The constant barrage of sights, sounds, and smells threatens to overwhelm him. He needs to get out of here, to find some semblance of peace and quiet before he makes an embarrassing scene.

He turns to Gatekeeper. "I need some air," he grumbles, his voice a low growl that's more beast than man.

The bouncer nods, his laser gaze never leaving the crowd. "Be careful out there, boss. That rain is weird. I could swear I heard it sizzling earlier. Seriously, what are we doing to the environment?"

As Paul steps out into the rain, the hot, almost gelatinous droplets offering an oddly comforting burn, he can't help but wonder if Gatekeeper's warning was more prophetic than he realized. Because he instinctively knows it's not just the rain that they have to fear.

It's each other.

Chapter 11

Back onstage, Bettie revels in the electric energy pulsating through the room as the crowd eagerly awaits the pièce de résistance of the evening: taunting Tristan, brandishing her whip with all the flair of a classic Lash LaRue-style striptease. With a roguish twinkle in her eye, Bettie joins Jayne, Rosie, and Marilyn—who's now wearing a faithful reproduction of the iconic *Some Like It Hot* white halter dress—in playfully mock-cowering from the flick of the whip, their laughter mingling with the crackle of anticipation in the air.

Tristan is in her element, fully immersed in the role, her movements fluid and precise as she expertly wields her prop with a balletic grace. Skating Rosie, ever the daredevil, attempts to catch the flick of the whip, but Tristan proves too quick for her, the supple end cracking just out of reach with tantalizing precision. Jayne, the epitome of fun, twirls away with a flourish, only to circle back for more, her eyes sparkling with spirited defiance. And then there's Bettie, embracing her inner feline as she mock-growls, her leopard-print wiggle dress hugging her curves with beguiling clinginess.

Amidst the whirlwind of activity, tragedy strikes in a flash of unexpected disorder. Newbie Marilyn, eager to prove herself, ventures too close and is inadvertently slashed in the face. With a pained gasp, she holds her hand to her eye, her exit from the stage overshadowed by the frenetic energy of the performance.

For Bettie, however, the incident barely registers. As the evening draws to a close and late night descends, she knows that the real money awaits in the private shows to come. Despite Rosie's wish to have Lipstick as her client tonight, it's Bettie who's been paired up with the familiar face. And truth be told, she couldn't be happier. Lipstick may not be the most glamorous client, but he's easy to deal with and always treats her with respect. Besides, he gives her practice in the art of makeup—Bettie doesn't plan on dancing forever. She wants to be a makeup artist for movies. Or maybe a screenwriter. Or… who knows?

The lights dim, casting the audience in shadow, but she can still feel their energy as a hum beneath her skin. She watches Tristan strut to the center, the crowd's applause a roar in her ears.

As a kid, Bettie fantasized about orchestrating behind those silver screens, pulling all the splendid strings. But let's face it, Hollywood's golden age went the way of the dinosaurs—if dinosaurs wore pancake makeup and starred in melodramas. Now, it's just a comic book blockbuster assembly line. And back then, finding a woman director was like getting a bargain on a unicorn at a used car lot. The era of the auteur? Ha, that sunk like a stone, thanks to an industry now led by market trends rather than artistic vision. The spooky slashers and Sundance sweethearts got swallowed whole by the insatiable streaming "content" monster.

Tristan's voice cuts through her thoughts. "And now," she purrs into the microphone, "let's give it up for our fabulously foxy cast!"

The spotlight swings back to them. Bettie joins Jayne and Rosie in a line, their smiles wide and genuine despite the long night. Jayne's eyes gleam with feisty fun as the headliner continues her banter.

"Jayne," Tristan coos with an impish grin, "she makes me go insane!"

The audience hoots and hollers, eating up every word.

"And Rosie," she continues with a wink, "always keeps me on my toes-ie!"

Laughter ripples through the crowd.

Tristan looks around with exaggerated consternation, then shrugs and says, "Where, oh where is Marilyn? Off to commit a sin?"

Bettie feels Tristan's gaze settle on her next. "And last but not least is our very own Bettie

Page," Tristan declares with a pause, "who's oh-so-pretty on this little stage!"

The crowd erupts again.

Bettie gives a small curtsy, glancing at Jayne, who rolls her eyes at the bad rhymes but can't hide her smile.

They take their final bows together, bound by their shared fondness for this wild world they inhabit—a realm far detached from Old Hollywood's elegance but overflowing with its own distinct draw... and an abundance of cleavage. As they leave the stage to the enduring applause of men with questionable intentions, Bettie realizes she'll continue to chase her cinematic dreams and embrace the unpredictability that follows. But for now, she's precisely where she belongs—sass, sparkles, and all.

* * *

Bettie notices the window has been left open again as they hang out backstage. Victor, who had been sitting on a chair earlier, is no longer there. Why wasn't he in his box? And where was the box? Did someone reach through the gap and steal him? Vintage dummies weren't cheap, even on eBay. Maybe Paul moved everything while tidying up the props, she muses, dismissing her worry for now.

Heading over to shut the window, Bettie catches sight of a strange, colorful light shimmering in the starless sky. For a moment, she wonders if it's an aurora borealis, though she knows it's unlikely in these city lights. Bettie watches with wide, apprehensive eyes as the storm outside grows more violent by the second. Suddenly, a blinding flash tears through the inky darkness, lightning shooting down from the heavens with fury. She can see each bolt crackling with an almost sentient energy as it arcs across the sky and strikes the ground with a deafening impact. The electric sparks dance menacingly along the earth, illuminating twisted shadows that seem to writhe and stretch toward her. Intrigued and slightly unsettled, she calls Jayne over to take a look, her voice tinged with curiosity.

Jayne saunters over, her interest piqued by Bettie's tone. Together, they peer up at the bizarre display, eyes widening in unison. After a brief, silent contemplation, they both agree that the colors—garish and clashing—are far too ugly to be an aurora borealis. Something else entirely is at play, and it sends a shiver rippling over Bettie's goose-fleshed skin.

"Must be smog and acid rain," Tristan guesses, joining them.

"Great," Rosie groans. "That's all I need, skating home. Bet there's oil slicks, too. Oh, joy!"

Bettie turns to her, surprised. "You're gonna skate? Isn't that dangerous?"

Rosie chuckles darkly. "Oh honey, you have no idea. Just last week, I was rolling home when some gang members started shooting at each other. Bullets whizzing by my head like hostile hornets."

The girls lean in, eyes narrowed with a mix of horror and fascination.

"But I just kept skating," Rosie continues, a glint of pride in her eye. "Blew right past them like a bat out of hell. They were so shocked that they forgot all about their little turf war."

Bettie shakes her head in disbelief. "Weren't you scared?"

"Scared? Nah." Rosie waves a dismissive hand. "When you've been skating these streets as long as I have, you learn to roll with the punches. Literally."

The girls chuckle, the tension broken by Rosie's nonchalant attitude toward the dangers of the city. Bettie decides that Irma must've opened the window for some air while waiting for the last act to end.

"Besides," Rosie adds with a shrug, "nothing gets the adrenaline pumping like a little brush with death. Keeps me young."

Chapter 12

Nestled in the shadows of the girls' dressing room, Paul seeks solace from the blinding flashes of light that dance across the stage. The pulsating music echoes faintly in the background, a distant reminder of the vibrant spectacle unfolding beyond the confines of his secluded sanctuary. But even in the relative quiet of the dressing room, Paul's unease festers like a wound left untended.

His gaze falls upon Marilyn as she enters the room, a faint cut marring the delicate skin below her eye. Though it's just a nick, Paul winces at the sight, his instinct to offer comfort warring with his desire to remain hidden in the shadows. Her eyes are so pretty, so blue, so… yummy-looking. He watches in silence as Marilyn tends to her wound, the soft rustling of fabric mingling with the strains of music from the stage.

But then, a second rustle breaks the fragile stillness of the room, drawing Marilyn's attention to the clothes rack. Paul tenses, his senses on high alert as he scans the dimly lit space for any sign of intrusion. Yet, to his relief—or perhaps disappointment—there's nothing to be seen, save for the eerie silhouettes of dress forms and the frozen-faced mannequins lurking in the shadows.

There's a squeak, then a tiny scuffle.

"Rats. Nice," Marilyn murmurs under her breath, her voice barely a whisper against the backdrop of the music.

As the dancer's attention shifts back to her reflection in the mirror, Paul's eyes dart to the still-closed window, his mind racing with thoughts of potential threats lurking just beyond the pane. But everything appears undisturbed. He turns back to gaze at Marilyn, but she's gone.

Paul's mind spins. She couldn't have just vanished. He had looked away for barely a heartbeat. His new, cursed hearing should have picked up the slightest noise, even her breath.

"Where the hell did she go?" he mutters, voice tinged with frustration and something else—worry.

His eyes dart to the window again, narrowing as they adjust to the moonlit darkness outside. There, partially obscured by a gnarled oak tree, a dark figure lurks. Paul's heart skips a beat. He watches as the stranger skulks from the side courtyard toward the street out front.

No one peeps for free. He won't tolerate it.

He staggers to his feet, muscles aching with the unfamiliar stiffness that has plagued him all evening. Each step feels like wading through molasses, but anger fuels his movements.

Bursting into the hallway, Paul stomps towards the front door, each stride echoing off the old wooden floors of the makeshift Fetish Factory. The rhythmic thud of his steps mingles with the distant music and laughter from the stage area, but his focus remains fixed on one thing: catching that damn peeper.

Paul throws open the door with a force that rattles its hinges. The humid air hits him like a slap, sharpening his senses even further. He scans the side courtyard, eyes locking onto the tree where he saw the figure moments ago.

"Show yourself!" he barks into the night, voice carrying an authority honed from years behind a camera lens and managing performers.

He waits, staring into the darkness, but to his dismay, there's no one there. Only the faint scent of rain and the distant hum of traffic accompany his solitary vigil.

With a sigh of resignation, Paul retreats back into the safety of the club, his senses on high alert as he watches Bettie, Jayne, Tristan, and Rosie take their bows onstage. Meanwhile, Irma addresses the special clients seated in the roped-off VIP area, her voice a sultry purr. "Lucky four-leaf clovers, you stay right where you are."

As the rest of the audience begins to filter out into the rainy night, Paul rushes to usher them out, his mind still reeling from the encounter outside.

* * *

Returning to the office, he finds solace in the familiar routine of counting the night's earnings. The clink of coins and the rustle of cash are comforting reminders of a tangible world amidst the swirling chaos of uncertainty.

Fast as The Flash, Irma has changed back into her black Beatnik cigarette pants and mock turtleneck sweater, and she has a colorful silk scarf over her coif. She joins Paul, looking at all the cash collected from the patrons tonight. In keeping with the retro vintage service they provide, they do not accept credit cards and certainly no app payments. It's all cash.

Paul's fingers glide over the cash, counting with practiced precision. The soft rustle of bills and the clink of coins provide a steady rhythm, soothing his frayed nerves. He hears the creak of the door and looks up, spotting Bettie, Jayne, and Rosie as they sweep into the room, their faces alight with anticipation.

Paul straightens, slipping the last bill into a neat stack. "Alright, ladies," he begins, "tonight's special clients are in for a treat, right?"

Jayne salutes and says, "Yessir!" She flops onto a chair and exhales a satisfied, "Whew! That was awesome. That whip act never fails to get my blood pumping."

Bettie swats at her playfully. "You sexy bitch, you stole the show again."

Tristan, her brow furrowed with concern, interjects, "Hey, where's Marilyn? I haven't seen her since the final bow."

Irma, momentarily diverting her attention from the task at hand, looks up and echoes Tristan's concern, "Yeah, where is she? I hope she's alright."

Bettie goes into her best Monty Python in a flawless English accent, "Oh, it was just a flesh wound. Nothing to worry about."

Jayne, her confidence in the new girl unwavering, reassures them, "Yeah, Irma, she nodded like she was okay when I last saw her."

Irma, with a nonchalant shrug, decides to assign Marilyn's role to the masochist. "Well, she must be around here somewhere. I'll give her to Whipping Boy. If she's late, he'll just think he's being punished. Alright, ladies, let's not dilly-dally. We have rooms full of men to entertain and more money to count."

Jayne, always the most enthusiastic girl, shouts, "Bring 'em on! Let's give them a night they'll never forget."

"Let's buzzzz," Rosie adds, holding up her riveter.

Paul turns to Tristan. "You're on cha-cha duty for a long-distance client tonight. Room six is all set up for you. Just turn on the camera and do your thing."

Tristan gives a thumbs-up and shakes her bosom.

With their assignments clear, the girls exchange glances and head to the dressing room.

Paul watches them go, feeling a mix of pride and anxiety churn within him. He knows the show must go on despite the unsettling events outside. His mind races back to Marilyn's sudden disappearance and that mysterious figure by the tree. But now's not the time to dwell on it.

Turning back to the coffee table, Paul forces himself to focus on organizing the remaining cash and preparing for any unexpected surprises that may come their way tonight. The Fetish Factory thrives on its unique brand of vintage allure and secrecy; Paul knows he can lean on Irma to help him now that the stage show is over and out.

As Bettie's voice echoes down the hallway—some cheeky line from an old film—Paul feels a flicker of hope amidst his worries. For now, they continue their charade under cover of night and flashing lights.

Part Three: Zombies Vs. Strippers

Chapter 13

Bettie cherishes the time she spends on stage performing, feeling a thrilling party-mix of empowerment and creativity as she captures the audience's attention. It's an exhilarating experience where the spotlight and music amplify her personas. However, it's the one-on-one interactions with customers where she truly thrives. These intimate moments aren't about physicality, as sex is strictly off-limits, but rather about the psychological interplay and the deep, often raw conversations that unfold.

For Bettie, these chit-chats aren't just a box to tick on her burlesque bingo card, oh no, they're her very own human safari. She watches the wild emotions and experiences with the keenness of a hawk in heels. This little obsession with the human zoo is both a job requirement and a personal hobby, like a macabre Pokémon Go. Bettie, with her natural flair for flirtation, can tease out a client's story quicker than you can say "G-string." It's in these moments, when she's knee-deep in someone else's psyche, that she truly feels like a cinematic detective. Or a therapist. Or a really nosy neighbor.

Her ultimate dream is to channel these encounters and insights into writing a screenplay, seeing all her experiences as valuable research. Bettie believes that the authenticity of characters comes from collecting a treasure trove of inspiration from her nightly interactions. This aspiration sustains her, providing a long-term goal that feels both meaningful and reachable. Through her screenplay, she hopes to not only achieve her own dreams but to create a work that resonates with the universal desire for connection and understanding that she observes every night at The Fetish Factory. That, and a boatload of cash.

Bettie's eyes, adorned with a sweeping layer of black liner, catch sight of Lipstick across the room, its romantic glow dimmed just enough to add an air of mystery. He's a vision of vintage elegance, from the sheen of his well-polished shoes to the crisp lines of his slacks and dress shirt, all perfectly accented by a bold blue tie.

Her temporary boudoir is a space that echoes the iconic Bettie Page photo shoot with Bunny Yeager back in '54. The walls are a dynamic display of leopard-print easy-peel wallpaper, while a plush, velvet chaise lounge, the color of ripe cherries, is positioned in front of a large, ornate vanity, its art deco design adding a touch of class. Bettie can't help but marvel at how Paul and Irma manage to transport so many props and furniture pieces from one pop-up to the next, making each location a cocktail of the new and the familiar.

The air is nuanced with anticipation, but she doesn't immediately rush over. Instead, she takes her time, finishing her routine with the confidence and teasing delay of someone who knows they're being watched, especially by someone with an eager and expectant gaze.

"Waiting long?" she asks with a twinkle in her eye as she approaches Lipstick. Her tone suggests it's a rhetorical question; they both know he's always early for their sessions.

"Not too long," Lipstick responds, the corners of his mouth lifting in an endearing, if somewhat wolfish, smile. "You were... captivating, as usual."

Bettie laughs, a rich sound that seems to pull them into a private world. "Only as usual? Oh, Lipstick," she pretend-protests, "you wound me! I strive for the extraordinary."

His bare-lipped smile grows. "Extraordinary doesn't cover it."

Taking a seat opposite him, Bettie's demeanor shifts into a more private gear for this part of their routine. She leans in close, allowing the client to catch the scent of her perfume, and pulls out a compact mirror and a tube of lipstick. The color is a bold red, a matching shade to the name he's chosen for himself.

"Ready for your transformation?" she teases, uncapping the cylinder with a well-practiced hand.

Lipstick nods, his face a mask of feigned solemnity that barely conceals the elation in his eyes. "This won't smear, will it?" Lipstick queries, though they've gone over this dance many times before.

"Darling, with me, makeup is armor," she says. "And armor never smears in battle."

Her hand is steady as she begins to outline his lips, transforming them with careful, precise strokes into a beacon that emulates her own painted mouth. Through the mirror, their eyes meet—a silent acknowledgment of their shared connection, one that goes beyond the makeup and the stage, touching on their understanding of each other's deeper needs, the unspoken words between them.

As she applies vividly pigmented blue eyeshadow to Lipstick's lids with expert precision, Bettie playfully flicks one of her feathered fans over his head, eliciting a squeal of delight from her friend. "Hold still, Ralphie, or I'll shoot your eye out," she warns, brandishing the makeup brush like an air rifle. Lipstick chuckles at the reference to the holiday staple.

"My kids love that movie," he remarks as Bettie continues to transform him with her magic touch. She takes pride in her ability to bring out the beauty in others and help them see themselves in a new and empowering light. And with Lipstick, it's always a joyous and collaborative process, a celebration of their shared appreciation of glamour and artifice.

"I loved the way you were talking to that little man onstage," Lipstick says, referring to Bettie's sassy and commanding banter with the club's wooden mascot. "You were so stern and authoritative. It was hot."

Bettie smiles at the compliment, her eyes sparkling with mischief. "Well, darling, when you've got a big personality like mine, you've got to know how to wield it like a weapon. And trust me, I'm always armed and dangerous." She briefly hopes that Victor has been found and is back in his box in the dressing room, then turns her thoughts back to the task at hand.

With a final sweep of her brush, Bettie completes the client's makeup, and the two of them admire their reflection in the mirror. Bettie snaps the compact closed and sits back to admire her work. "Perfect. You're fit to take on the world now, my dear."

Lipstick purses his freshly embellished lips, amused. "Thanks to you," he says, slipping her a generous tip. "See you next week?"

"Wouldn't miss it for the world," Bettie replies, tucking the cash into her copious cleavage with a grateful nod. She stands up, ready to get back into her street clothes and on her way home, finally, but not before giving Lipstick's shoulder an affectionate squeeze. "Same time, another place."

As she sashays away, she knows Lipstick watches her performance continue, the art of putting on makeup now an act that transcends vanity, becoming instead a shared ritual, an intimate moment of companionship in their otherwise separate lives.

* * *

As Bettie descends the ancient, groaning staircase, she pauses to take off her pumps. But the well-trod carpet beneath her feet offers little comfort. The lights flicker ominously, accompanied by the unsettling sound of electrical zaps. This historical building may have its charms, but the last thing she needs to contend with at this late hour is an electrical fire. Then again, compared to the wild and peculiar experiences she's had working at The Fetish Factory, an electrical fire would be a walk in the park.

She inhales deeply, the musty scent of the runner mingling with the fresh, petrichor-laden aroma of the rain outside. But there's another smell, one that's animalistic and primal, that she can't quite pinpoint. It's unnerving, but she quashes her budding unease, her mind fixed on clocking out and heading home.

After all, she'll be spending most of the day in bed, but come evening, the New Beverly Cinema is screening *Ms. 45*, one of her all-time favorite grindhouse flicks. Bettie can't help but smile at the thought of the New Beverly Cinema, that glorious relic of a bygone era. Sure, the threadbare velvet seats squeak with every shift of her weight, and the popcorn is inevitably stale, the butter congealed into sludge. But that's all part of the experience, the magic of being transported to another world on that vast silver screen.

The prints may be washed out, scratchy, and imperfect, but that only adds to the draw. She could easily watch these cult classics in the comfort of her apartment, the movies painstakingly restored to pristine quality on Blu-ray. But there's something about seeing them projected in all their gritty, grainy glory, surrounded by fellow cinephiles—well, maybe not surrounded; more like sprinkled—who share her passion that simply can't be replicated.

As the opening credits roll, she'll sink into that creaky chair, the familiar scent of artificial butter lingering in the air, and let the flickering images whisk her away. For those precious hours, she'll be transported to a different realm.

The only thing missing is a partner to share these experiences with. Someone who'll understand the thrill of watching a battered 35mm print, who won't mind her quoting along with every line, someone whose hand she can clutch during the terrifying moments, whose shoulder she can burrow into when the tension becomes too much to bear.

Bettie chides herself for such sappy thoughts, rolling her eyes at her own sentimentality. She shakes her head, refocusing as she makes her way to the main dressing room.

Chapter 14

The slouchy sofa offers little comfort as Paul sinks into its worn cushions, his mind swimming with a brew of anxiety and bewilderment. Irma's voice cuts through the haze, her words sharp and decisive, but Paul struggles to grasp their meaning amidst the fog of his own turmoil.

"Has anyone found Marilyn yet? I swear, I checked that girl's references up the yin-yang. I don't hire flakes, and I'm never wrong," Irma declares, her tone tinged with frustration.

"You're never wrong," Paul parrots mechanically, his voice barely above a whisper as he wrestles with the mounting sense of unease nibbling at his insides.

"Not in all these years," Irma asserts, her confidence unwavering.

"Not in all these years," Paul repeats, a hollow echo of a truth he can no longer comprehend. His words come slowly and one at a time, like ice cubes falling from a rickety dispenser. Something is wrong—terribly wrong—but he can't seem to grasp the threads of reality as they slip away.

Irma's lighter snaps open with a metallic clang, the flame leaping high as it ignites the tip of her cigarillo. The sound reverberates through the room like a thunderclap, setting Paul's nerves on edge. He winces at the brightness, his eyes stinging with a sudden burst of pain that threatens to engulf him in its fiery embrace.

With a desperate gasp, Paul staggers to his feet and stumbles toward the door, his senses reeling from the onslaught of sensations assaulting him from all sides. He can feel Irma's stare on his back but he absolutely *must* get some air. And maybe some rain... the soft, warm, colorful rainfall beckons him for some reason.

As he steps into the hallway, his gaze falls upon Whipping Boy, the customer's figure bathed in shadow, his attention drawn to... what? The client listens intently at one of the doors, his riding whip clutched tightly in his grasp.

Suddenly, a sinister figure looms in the darkness, all stealth and menace, creeping ever closer to Whipping Boy with silent intent. Is it the mysterious figure from before, or something even more sinister? Paul's heart, which feels oddly slow and weak, pulses as he watches, paralyzed with fear and morbid curiosity. He stays quiet.

Suddenly, the client turns, his gasp of surprise echoing through the hallway.

It's Gatekeeper, his features twisted in confusion and alarm as he confronts what he thought was an intruder with a mixture of apprehension and defiance. "What are you doing?" he demands.

"I, uh... sorry. Nothing. I was just waiting for Marilyn—" Whipping Boy's words are cut short as chaos erupts in a flurry of violence and terror.

An undead mob descends upon Gatekeeper with savage ferocity, their white-eyed gazes burning with a hunger that chills Paul to the bone. He stands frozen in place, his mind a whirlwind of differing emotions as he watches the scene unfold before him. Part of him longs to join in the fray, to unleash the pent-up fury and frustration that simmers beneath the surface of his stoic façade. But another part recoils in horror at the sight of the carnage before him, a visceral reminder of the fragility of life and the depths of darkness that lurk.

As the lead creature's grotesque form lunges forward, its maw yawning wide in a twisted mockery of hunger, Paul's world tilts on its axis, his hold on reality slipping through his fingers like sand. The monster is doing a series of kicks, leaps, and arm movements. The absurdity of it all should be laughable—a zombie, of all things, performing martial arts!—but the scene unfurling before him is nothing short of a waking nightmare. He stands rooted to the spot, his eyes wide with disbelief as the undead creature executes a series of moves with a grace that belies its decaying form.

Paul is no martial artist; he's always been more of a sedentary man, preferring the quiet hum of his work to the uproar of the world outside, but he's seen enough Bruce Lee movies to recognize the fluidity of Shaolin technique. Yet, as the undead man's bones crunch and grind with each leap and kick, he can't help but shudder at the horrific sight.

Kung Fu Zombie's dance of death is a horrifying spectacle to behold. Its limbs move with a sickening fluidity, its cartilage cracking and grinding with each leap and kick. The air is thick with the stench of decay as the creature performs a macabre ballet, its movements a bizarre parody of life.

Paul watches in horror as the zombie's face contorts into a twisted leer, its white eyes burning with a hunger that chills him to the bone. Now he recognizes the figure before him—it's one of the audience men from earlier, transformed into this abomination. The realization sends a shiver down his spine, and he can't help but feel a sense of dread creeping into his bones. *Is this my future?*

As Kung Fu Zombie continues its deadly dance, Paul feels a strange sensation coursing through his veins. It's as if something is stirring within him, awakening a primal instinct that he's never known existed. He feels a sudden surge of strength, his muscles tensing with a power that he can't explain.

But with this newfound strength comes a terrifying realization. Paul is changing. His mind is not able to keep track of many thoughts at once, and his senses are heightened to a level that is both invigorating and terrifying. He can barely hear now, and his vision has lost its faculty for details, but he sees even the slightest movement in the darkest of shadows, and he can smell the scent of fear emanating from the other occupants of The Fetish Factory.

As Kung Fu Zombie's cavorting reaches its climax, Paul feels a sudden urge to join the creature. His body moves of its own accord, his limbs flailing wildly as he stumbles forward, his eyes locked on the grotesque figure before him. He can feel the hunger burning within him, a primal desire to feed on human flesh.

But just as he is about to lunge at Whipping Boy, Gatekeeper, and Kung Fu Zombie, a sudden jolt of recognition hits him like a bolt of lightning. It's Irma who pulls him back from the brink, her strong arms wrapping around him as she whispers words of reassurance in his ear.

"Stay back," she whispers, her voice a soothing balm to his tortured mind.

Paul clings to her, his body trembling with fear and relief. As he looks into Irma's dark brown eyes, he can see the same fear and uncertainty reflected back at him.

Together, they watch as the Kung Fu Zombie collapses to the ground, its body convulsing with an agonizing spasm. Paul knows that they are not safe—not by a long shot. But for now, they have each other, and that's enough. They stand in the doorway between their office and the hallway, watching and waiting.

Around them, horror reigns supreme. Whipping Boy's piercing screams echo through the air as he flees for the relative safety of the upstairs rooms, while Gatekeeper stands firm, his expression a mask of grim determination as he faces off against the undead atrocity. And yet, despite the havoc that swirls around him, Paul can only stand and watch, clutching onto Irma, his body frozen with shock as a bizarre and inexplicable scene unfolds before his bleary eyes.

Chapter 15

Tristan, Jayne, and Bettie shuffle into the dressing room. Jayne's laughter rings out in blunt contrast to Bettie's weary sigh.

"That was fun," Jayne giggles, her voice laced with the remnants of excitement. She sits down at the vanity, ready to strip off her war paint.

Bettie, her exhaustion palpable, stifles a yawn. "Yeah, long night, though."

"I am so ready to get paid and go home," Tristan declares, her tone a blend of relief and impatience.

The sentiment is echoed by the others as they nod in agreement.

Bettie's gaze falls upon Rosie, huddled by the side door, rhythmically and agitatedly spinning her skates beneath her. Something is wrong.

"Rosie, are you okay?" Bettie's concern is met with an almost imperceptible, trembling nod from the obviously terrified mime.

A faint ringing sound cuts through the air, drawing Bettie's attention away from Rosie's crouched form. As if by an unseen force, her notice is pulled to the area behind the clothing rack. The sight that greets her there is one of pure, unadulterated horror.

Marilyn's lifeless body is crumpled on the floor, her eyes disturbingly absent from their sockets, leaving behind bloody, gaping voids.

"Oh my god! What the fuck?" The words tumble out of Bettie's mouth in a breathless rush, her mind reeling with shock and disbelief.

Tristan, her voice trembling with caution, is the first to speak. "She's... um, I think she's dead." The statement hangs in the air, a grim acknowledgment of the reality before them.

Jayne, ever the picture of nonchalance, rises from her seat with a practiced grace. She adjusts her garter, her eyes casually surveying the scene before her. "Who?" she asks, her tone deceptively casual. But then her eyes settle on Marilyn's lifeless form, and her expression shifts. "Yeah, she's dead. Looks like she O.D.'ed."

Bettie's heart pounds in her chest, a wild drumbeat that echoes the bedlam of her thoughts. "What? Did you see her eyes?" she demands with disbelief. She gestures towards the gore-soaked craters, unable to find the words to articulate the awfulness of the sight.

Jayne shrugs, her demeanor oddly detached. "Yeah, so? Who knows what the drugs are doing these days?" Her words are a dismissive wave, an attempt to brush away the stark reality of their situation.

But Bettie refuses to accept such an explanation. With a resolute shake of her head, she regains her composure, her eyes hardening with resolve. "I guess we'd better tell Irma and Paul we found her," she declares, her voice firm despite the tremor of confusion that lingers beneath the surface.

Tristan recoils at the suggestion, her voice heavy with horror. "Uh, how about 9-1-1?" The question is a plea, a desperate attempt to cling to the safety and security of the world they once knew.

But Bettie shakes her head, her resolve unwavering. "No way. That's not our call. Let's tell Irma and Paul and see what they want to do." She puts on her big girl shoes and starts to lead the way.

Leaving Rosie behind, the trio rushes through the connecting door into the manager's office, seeking guidance from the nightmare unfolding before them.

But what they discover inside is a tableau of such horrendous violence that it surpasses their wildest notions. Paul and The Gatekeeper, once trusted comrades, now stand hunched over Irma's lifeless form, their mouths glistening with crimson droplets as they tear at her ravaged flesh. Her eye sockets are hollows of viscera, a chilling witness to the abominations that have seized them.

The women reel back in utter terror, their piercing screams reverberating through the chamber, bouncing off the cold, unfeeling walls. Shadows play a devilish dance along the surfaces, their forms warping and twisting with each fleeting second, as if echoing the tumult in their minds. The relentless drumming of the rainstorm outside merges with the erratic hum of the flickering lights and the guttural growls of the encroaching creatures, weaving a thread of dread that seeps into their very marrow.

Bettie's throat constricts as she struggles to comprehend the ghastly scene before her. Jayne and Tristan huddle behind her, their panicked breaths melding with the endless patter of the downpour.

"This... this can't be real," Bettie stammers, her voice barely audible above the rain's relentless percussion.

Jayne's hands fly to her mouth, muffling a strangled sob. "Oh, honey, I think we've stumbled into a real-life *Night of the Living Dead.*"

"Welcome to hell, motherfuckers!" Bettie says with a mirthless chuckle.

Tristan's eyes widen, and she whispers, "Zombies? Like, actual, real-live zombies?"

Bettie's mind races, attempting to reconcile the absurdity of their situation with the undeniable horror unfolding in front of them. "We need to get out of here," she declares, her voice regaining some of its earlier resolve.

The trio inches backward, their hearts pounding in sync with the thunderous crashes outside. The zombified Paul and The Gatekeeper snarl, their bloodstained faces contorting into grotesque masks of hunger.

"Maybe if we just, you know, tiptoe away, they won't notice us," Jayne suggests, her voice quivering.

Bettie shakes her head, her eyes never straying from the monstrous figures before her. "No way. We need to make a run for it."

As if on cue, a streak of lightning illuminates the room, casting a stark, eerie glow upon the women's faces. The zombies' growls intensify, and they cover their faces until the light subsides. Then they advance, their gnarled hands reaching out toward the potential feast before them.

"For God's sake, girls, get out," Bettie whispers, her voice laced with a steely determination that belies her fear.

With a collective gasp, the trio turns and bolts toward the door, their heels clattering against the nicked floor. The zombies' snarls echo behind them.

Bursting through the exit, they find themselves in the dimly lit hallway, the shadows casting an ominous pall over their surroundings.

"Which way?" Tristan pants, her eyes darting wildly around the corridor.

Bettie hesitates, her mind frantically searching for an escape route. "I... I'm not sure. We need to find a way out of here, but we can't risk running into more of those... things."

Jayne's eyes narrow, and she points toward a door at the end of the hall. "What's behind that door, Betts? It's our only option."

Bettie's gaze follows Jayne's pink-nailed finger, her heart hammering in her chest. "I think it's the storage room. But it could be another way out."

The dancers exchange anxious glances, the weight of their decision pressing upon them. The cacophony surrounds them, a relentless reminder of the chaos that now governs their lives.

"We've got to chance it," Bettie says finally, her voice a mere croak above the storm's din. "It's our only hope. Let's go get Rosie."

As they scramble back toward the dressing room, their hearts throbbing violently against their ribs, they realize with a jolt that they are not alone.

Another zombie lies in wait in the gloom, its snarling face bathed in the weak, ghostly light of the moonbeam filtering through the window. The creature, dressed in a purple dress shirt and pressed jeans, staggers blindly in the dim light, a grotesque parody of a man Bettie had seen from onstage only a couple of hours before. His once-handsome face is now a mask of malice, his eyes vacant and lifeless.

As the women huddle together, their breaths coming in ragged gasps, the zombie seems unaware of their presence. He sways unsteadily, his movements jerky and uncoordinated, as if struggling to maintain his balance. His head lolls to one side, and for a moment, Bettie thinks he is going to collapse to the floor.

But then, with a sudden burst of strength, the abomination lurches towards the door, his arms outstretched. He stumbles over the threshold, his body colliding with the wall on the other side with a sickening thud. The women watch in horrified silence as he disappears into the darkness of the hallway, his guttural moans resonating in their ears.

Bettie's heart gallops in her chest as she tries to make sense of what she has just witnessed. The zombie seemed so weak and disoriented. It was as if he was not fully in control of his own body, as if some other force was guiding him. And then there was the fact that he had not attacked them. The women had been within arm's reach of the creature, and yet he had shown no interest in them. It was as if he was focused on something else, something that had drawn him away from the dressing room door and into the depths of the club.

Bettie's mind races with possibilities, her thoughts a chaotic jumble of fear and flummox. But one thing is clear: they cannot stay here. They must find a way to escape, to get away from the horrors that have overtaken The Fetish Factory.

"Where'd he go?" Bettie gasps, her breaths coming in ragged gasps as she struggles to comprehend the scene unfolding before her.

"I don't know," Jayne mutters, her voice trembling as she scans the room. "But come on, let's go get Rosie."

As Bettie scrambles to formulate a plan, she can't resist the temptation to quip, "If anyone asks, I'm the plucky heroine, not the first one to die, because I refuse to be upstaged by a bunch of extras with worse makeup than mine!"

Jayne and Tristan shake their heads but smile in spite of themselves.

Circumventing the office, they tiptoe through the hallway by the stairs and re-enter the dressing room. They close the door and turn the lock.

Rosie, who'd so recently bragged about her fearlessness with the gauntlet of gang members she'd rolled by the other night, is still huddled on the floor. Marilyn's ravaged dead body hadn't gone anywhere, either.

Outside the door, the faint snarls of approaching zombies grow louder, their relentless appetites driving them ever closer to their prey. The door rattles as they pound against it, their inhuman strength threatening to break through at any moment.

"So, who wants to call the cops now?" Tristan asks with exasperation.

"Yeah, call them," Jayne agrees.

But their hopes are dashed when Tristan admits, "I didn't bring my phone. It's too tempting, so I left it at home."

Jayne's frown deepens as she realizes, "Me, too."

"All's I've got is my iPod," Bettie offers, her voice barely above a whisper. "It's in my locker. Can't make calls from it, anyway."

Their eyes turn toward their colleague's lifeless form in the corner of the room, her phone clutched in her hand like a lifeline. The sight is enough to make Bettie's heart race, a cold sweat prickling her brow. Rosie, the closest to the phone, shakes her head, her fear palpable and her face ashen.

With a resigned sigh, Jayne steps forward, her movements slow and hesitant as she approaches the body. Bettie watches her friend with a concoction of dread and hope, her breath catching in her throat. What if Marilyn comes back to life? Jayne's hands tremble as she pries the device from Marilyn's stiff fingers, then runs as fast as she can with her tight skirt.

She dials the trio of digits, her eyes laser-focused as she punches in the numbers. "It's ringing!" she announces.

But their hopes are shattered when a recording plays, "We are sorry. All circuits are busy. Please try your call again." The mechanical voice echoes in the tense air, a cruel confirmation of their dilemma.

Bettie's heart sinks, the weight of their predicament pressing down on her soul. She exchanges a glance with Jayne, the shared panic in their eyes deepening the sense of despair that hangs in the room. Jayne presses a few more buttons, desperately searching for a signal. Bettie can see the frustration and fear sketched on her friend's face as the phone remains silent, its screen displaying nothing but static.

"Well, that's another fine mess you've got me into, Ollie," Bettie mutters, her sarcasm a feeble try to quiet the jumbling of her gut.

Jayne tosses the phone aside, her eyes scanning the room for any other means of escape. "We need to barricade the door," she says.

Rosie, who's still crouched in the corner, whimpers in agreement.

"Yes," Tristan says.

Bettie nods, her mind racing as she tries to come up with another plan. The room is small, cluttered with costumes and makeup. A single window offers a glimmer of hope but there are more monsters outside than inside. Her eyes land on a sturdy-looking wardrobe.

"Let's move that," Bettie suggests, her voice steady despite her growing panic.

The three women spring into action, their muscles straining as they push the weighty piece of furniture toward the door. The growls outside are growing louder, the door rattling against its hinges.

Bettie strains, her breaths coming in ragged gasps. "Looks like I picked the wrong week to quit sniffing glue."

With a final heave, they manage to wedge the wardrobe against the door, the rattling ceasing for a moment—only to be redoubled as the creatures outside realize they've been stymied.

The women huddle together as they try to come up with a plan. The growls outside are growing louder, the wardrobe shaking against the door.

Bettie thinks of her mother, of the movies they used to watch together. She thinks of the strong, fearless femme fetales on the screen, their determination and bravery in the face of danger. She casts a furtive glance at Jayne, Tristan, and Rosie, their faces etched with shock. In that moment, a stray thought flits through her mind, a fleeting moment of levity.

"Well, at least I'm not the big-breasted blonde who always dies first in those eighties slasher flicks," she muses with a wry smile. A soft chuckle escapes her lips, a momentary release of the tension that grips her body.

Jayne shoots her a quizzical look. "What's so funny?" she hisses, her voice a harsh whisper. "You *are* a big-breasted blonde!"

Bettie shakes her head, her smile broadening. "Sure, but that they don't know that." She pats her black wig. "And I was just thinking about how grateful I am that my girls aren't quite as... ample as yours. Might just give me a fighting chance against these undead freaks."

Jayne's eyes widen in realization, and despite the gravity of their situation, a faint smile tugs at her mouth. "You're such a bitch," she murmurs, but there's no malice in her words, only a hint of grudging admiration.

For a brief moment, the two women share a knowing look, a silent acknowledgment of the absurdity of their circumstances.

The wardrobe shudders violently, the ruckus growing more insistent, more desperate. Bettie's heart skips a beat, the severity of their situation crashing back.

"Okay, ladies," she says, her voice low and steady. "Let's figure out a way out of this mess before one of us ends up as the next victim in this real-life horror marathon." Bettie straightens her back. "We're getting out of here," she concludes, her voice steady and sure.

Chapter 16

To their surprise, Marilyn's phone rings again, its shrill tone cutting through the silence like a dagger. Jayne dives for it, her eyes wide with disbelief as she answers the call.

"Hello?" she whispers, her voice trembling with fear. Then, "Hello? Hello?" She looks at her friends. "Nobody's there."

Tristan demands, "Who was it? Could you see who it was? Does the phone still work? Call 9-1-1 again," she urges, her voice filled with desperation as she clings to the slim hope of salvation from the outside.

A somber silence falls over the room, broken only by Jayne's mournful words. "I think it's dead," she says sadly, gesturing toward the lifeless device in her hand. But then, her expression changes as she notices something on the screen. "But look…"

An image of the caller fills the screen, a snapshot frozen in time, capturing a moment of happiness. It's Marilyn and a handsome young man, his arm wrapped around her in a loving embrace.

"Must be her boyfriend," Jayne speculates, holding the phone up for everyone to see.

Their expressions grow melancholy as they contemplate the fate of their own loved ones. Will they ever see them again?

The phone makes a strange noise; Jayne reads, frowns, and then says, "Just news about the storm. Yeah, we know!" Jayne sighs. "Betts is right. We can't stay here. We need to get out, get help."

Rosie pipes up. "Are you crazy? I'm not going out there! Did you happen to notice our, um, friend... there on the floor? I like my eyes just where they are, thank you."

An argument erupts between Jayne and Rosie, their voices rising in frustration and fear.

Bettie leans against one of the mannequins, anything for support. She twirls a lock of raven hair around her finger and takes in Marilyn's lifeless body slumps against the wall, her vacant eye sockets staring into nothingness, a wordless witness to the evil that has befallen The Fetish Factory.

"Look, Rosie," Bettie begins, "we're not in Kansas anymore." She gestures toward the window where the guttural groans of the undead drift in with the smell of rain turned sour. "And those aren't fans begging for an encore."

Jayne nods in agreement, her usually vibrant eyes dulled by the grim reality. "We don't know why they're here or how to stop them, but one thing's for sure—those zombie dudes aren't here for The Fetish Factory VIP meet-and-greet."

Rosie's arms are wrapped tight around herself as if the gesture could ward off their nightmare. She shudders, casting a fearful glance at the lifeless mannequins standing sentinel around them—now less creepy than what lurks beyond their semi-safe haven.

"Zombies? Really?" Rosie's voice is laced with incredulity and a touch of hysteria. "What is this, one of your stupid B-movies come to life?"

Bettie chuckles dryly, "Honey, if this were a movie, I'd be demanding better lighting and a script rewrite." Her eyes dart to Marilyn's body again. "I'm sure you'd agree."

Bettie, Jayne, and Tristan stand in a triangle of uncertainty, surrounded by racks of costumes and props that once represented escape but now seem like artifacts from another life. The scent of latex and leather mingles with the acrid stench seeping in from outside—a stark reminder that their reality has shifted into overdrive.

"We need a plan," Bettie stresses, tapping her chin thoughtfully. "Preferably one that doesn't involve us becoming an all-you-can-eat buffet."

Jayne sighs and glances toward the window again. The moans grow louder as shadows pass by—the undead shuffling aimlessly through the storm-soaked side yard. "And soon," she adds quietly.

Rosie's eyes flit between Bettie and Jayne before settling on Marilyn once more. Her expression softens with grief for their fallen friend. "Alright," she concedes with a trembling breath. "Let's figure this out—without becoming zombie chow." Finally, she gets to her feet. Or wheels, as the case may be.

Meanwhile, Tristan takes action, grabbing a tiara and breaking it into pieces to use as makeshift weapons. "I can use these as ninja stars. Plus, I have my whip," she says defiantly, ready to fight whatever comes their way.

Jayne goes to the opposite door and peers cautiously out into the dark office. She turns back to her colleagues, whispering, "I think it's okay."

Tristan approaches, her bullwhip coiled and her other hand clutching the rhinestone crown pieces.

Without warning, Jayne and Tristan are yanked from the room, their surprised cries echoing in the confined space. Bettie's heart hammers as she watches in horror, frozen for a split second before her instincts kick in. The shadows beyond the door seem to writhe with malevolent intent, and her thoughts race, frantically trying to gain traction. Every muscle in her body tenses, ready to spring into action, but the oppressive darkness makes it impossible to see what had taken them—and where.

Bettie and Rosie huddle together, their pulses pounding as they watch the other zombies shamble past the window. Bettie's mind races, struggling to grasp the reality of the situation. It can't be real, she thinks desperately. That's it! Like the *Wizard of Oz*, it's all a dream. Or did the bartender slip her a Mickey Finn? The thought is absurd, but right now, nothing makes sense.

The sound of breaking glass shatters her wishful illusions. Rotten, elongated, clawed hands reach through the shattered window, grasping at the sill with blind gropes.

With no other options left, Bettie grabs and brandishes a nearly empty whiskey bottle, ready to defend herself against whatever horrors lie beyond the door. She unscrews the top, then downs whatever liquid courage might be left. "As Bluto said in *Animal House*, 'My advice to you: start drinking heavily!'"

She chins toward the wardrobe and tells Rosie they've got to move it—obviously, going out the door to the office didn't work out so well for their pals.

Once done, Rosie reaches for her riveter, a newfound determination in her eyes. But then she screams, dropping her weapon. Bettie gasps and flattens herself against the nearest wall.

Jayne propels herself into the dressing room from the office, her golden hair a mess and with a large, bleeding scratch across one cheek. "Tristan's gone," she sobs, holding up the bullwhip, which has been torn to shreds.

"Oh, fuck…" Bettie whispers. "The smart brunet dies. These zombies are flipping the script on us."

Jayne, her camera still hanging from its strap around her neck, holds the device up and looks at it with wonder. "I accidentally flashed," she says. "They didn't like that. They stopped attacking, and I… um, just me… I got away." She wipes a tear, then looks at herself in the mirror. She traces the claw mark on her cheek with her index finger. Shaking her head as if to clear it, she turns around and then takes off her garter belt.

"What's wrong?" Bettie asks. "Feeling overdressed?"

"Ha, ha," Jayne replies. "No, I'm gonna use it as a slingshot." She grabs some perfume bottles from the vanity, preparing to use them as ammunition.

Rosie retrieves her riveter, and Bettie gets a good grip on the neck of her bottle. With their makeshift arsenal in hand, the women steel themselves for what lies ahead.

* * *

They venture out and immediately, Bettie hears male chatter. She draws back, listening. It's not zombie babble; it's human voices. She tiptoes down the hall, motioning for the others to stay close and quiet. The speakers are nearby. She follows the sound, and then she sees the "lucky four-leaf clovers."

Footman, The Flasher, Whipping Boy, and Lipstick are huddled behind some chairs in the burlesque room. They seem just as uneasy as Bettie feels. The flickering lights and swaying shadows only add to the eerie atmosphere, making it difficult to discern friend from foe.

Bettie watches the customers with a blend of trepidation and suspicion. What if they're monsters? Or on the verge of transforming into something sinister? They don't appear threatening, but she isn't willing to take any chances. Motioning for Rosie and Jayne to stay back, she cautiously approaches the group alone, her heart flip-flopping.

Lipstick, with his bold makeup and an unlit flashlight, tries to rally the group. He doesn't see Bettie, so she decides to hang back and eavesdrop a bit longer. It seems to her that they're ducking the undead too, but she's not taking any chances.

"We can't hide in here all night," Lipstick points out, his voice tense.

Footman nods in agreement, his face etched with concern that mirrors the gravity of their situation. Beside him, Whipping Boy's unease is palpable; he shifts his weight from one foot to the other, and in doing so, his movement sends a chair off-kilter, its loud scraping noise reverberating off the hardwood floor. The sharp sound slices through the strained silence, causing everyone to freeze in place. Bettie feels her breath catch in her throat as they all stand statue-still, ears alert, listening for the slightest hint of peril that might be stalking them just beyond their sight.

There's nothing. Even the distant cries have abated.

"How do we do this?" The Flasher whispers anxiously, his eyes darting toward the front door. "Let's just make a break for it."

Lipstick's gaze falls on an inert form lying near the threshold. "Yeah, you can see how well that worked for whoever that is," he remarks callously.

Bettie bristles at his disregard for the person lying unconscious by the door. *What a bunch of cowards*, she thinks, her opinion of the men sinking.

Whipping Boy checks his watch, his anxiety unmistakable. "My wife is going to kill me," he mutters under his breath. "What about the girls?" he asks.

Finally, Bettie thinks.

"They've got to be dead by now. We have to look out for ourselves!" Lipstick clenches his fists in determination. "Come on, let's go," he declares, picking up the flashlight and turning it on.

Whipping Boy, less enthusiastic about facing whatever lies beyond the safety of the room, voices his reluctance. "Okay, but I'm only kicking ass if I really have to. If I see an open door and freedom, I'm outta here."

Bettie's heart tightens as Lipstick's words carve through the tension in the air, each syllable a traitorous sting. Here she is, overhearing a conversation she wishes were just another scripted exchange from one of her cherished films, yet here the betrayal cuts deeper than any on-screen drama.

She always thought Lipstick liked her; their banter during shows had been a highlight of her nights. But as his flippant dismissal of their potential fate hangs in the air, she realizes that the camaraderie was as superficial as the makeup that still clings impeccably to his lying face. Even amidst an apocalypse, his eyeliner doesn't smudge, and his lipstick doesn't bleed—a perfect façade that now seems to amplify their superficial connection.

So much for gratitude, she muses bitterly. Bettie had danced for them, laughed with them, made their evenings something to remember. And yet, when faced with life and death, it appears the only thing Lipstick cares to consider is his own survival.

Her feelings bruised but her spirit still ablaze with sarcasm, Bettie suppresses a snort. Oh, what a knight in shimmering foundation he turned out to be! She imagines sniping at him about loyalty being more than skin-deep—less durable than his no-budge makeup, apparently.

She decides then, with a searing clarity that surprises even herself, to remain hidden in the shadows. Let them think she's one of the unlucky ones—just another victim of this terrible scenario. Bettie is no damsel in distress waiting for rescue by men who can barely muster the courage to face reality. She hopes they enjoy their own personal *Fright Night*.

As Lipstick's flashlight beam slices through the darkness, threatening to reveal her hiding spot, Bettie presses further back against the wall. Her body tenses like a coiled spring, ready to unleash a sharp retort or fend off any undead—or ungrateful—advance.

Jayne catches her eye from across the room; there's an unspoken understanding between them. Her gaze flickers with shared indignation but also with that fire of resilience both the bombshell and the pinup queen harbor within.

They don't need saving. Not by Lipstick or any other self-serving soul who wanders through The Fetish Factory's doors. They'll write their own script tonight—one where they aren't reduced to mere background characters in someone else's escape plan. Bettie clenches her fist, feels the weight of the whiskey bottle, and steels herself for what comes next. She'll survive—and she'll do it on her own terms.

With a mixture of fear and determination, she watches as the four men tiptoe toward the bar area, their shadows dancing against the walls as they move.

Bettie retreats unseen and silent to the hallway, where Rosie and Jayne await.

Chapter 17

As they look toward the front door, contemplating their next move, Rosie whispers, "I have an idea."

Bettie and Jayne lean in, eager to hear Rosie's plan, hoping it might offer them even a sparkle of hope in their dire situation.

Bettie's heart races as Rosie outlines her plan. The idea of the slender redhead on roller skates, darting through the darkness like a streak of lightning, fills her with varied emotions. But what choice do they have?

"It's our best shot," she agrees, her voice shaky with apprehension. "But please, Rosie, be careful. We need you back here." She looks down the long hallway and to the front door. The body that had been lying there is gone... *Great. Probably resurrected and reanimated*, she thinks darkly.

Jayne nods in agreement, her expression mirroring Bettie's concern. "If it's safe, come right back. We'll all go together. If not, then keep going—straight to the police station. We need the SWAT team here."

With a resolute nod, Rosie begins to psyche herself up, the wheels of her roller skates oscillating back and forth in eager anticipation. In half a heartbeat, she launches herself forward, each powerful stride propelling her further into the eerie darkness that envelops the hallway.

Bettie's breath hitches in her throat as she watches Rosie's silhouette hurtle towards the front door, a hint of hope rising within her. For a fleeting moment, it seems as though Rosie might just make it, that she will actually breach the threshold of safety and freedom. But just as that thought crosses Bettie's mind, a monstrous figure materializes from the shadows, its gnarled hands lunging out to seize Rosie in its vice-like grip.

Bettie's heart plummets as she witnesses Rosie's desperate struggle, the riveter in her hand swinging wildly in a futile attempt to break free. The sheer strength of the attacker's hold is overwhelming, and with a heavy, sinking feeling plummeting to her aching feet, Bettie realizes that their best plan for escape has been cruelly thwarted. As the creature sinks its teeth into Rosie's throat and then goes for her eyes, Bettie can't bear to watch any longer.

Still clutching her whiskey bottle, she grabs Jayne's hand, and they retreat back into the dressing room. The sight of Marilyn's lifeless body is too much to bear, so they contemplate the multiple exits—each room had several doors to connect the mazelike layout—then make their way into the adjoining jack-and-jill bathroom, slamming the door shut behind them.

The tiny space offers a brief respite—its walls almost a hug. As the girls huddle together, the fading grandeur of the art deco style surrounds them. The once-elegant room now wears a veneer of neglect, its pink-painted walls peeling and stained with watermarks from years of neglect. The floor tiles, previously pristine, now bear the scars of countless spike-heeled footsteps and are cracked and chipped in places. In the center stands a clawfoot tub, its porcelain gleam dulled by time and neglect. An opaque shower curtain hangs around it, its pattern faded and worn from years of use. Beside the tub, a pedestal sink stands, its once-gleaming surface now tarnished and marred with age. Despite the dilapidation, there's a strange comfort in the well-worn feel of the surroundings.

Bettie's tears mingle with the echoes of dripping water as she tries to make sense of what they've witnessed. "What are those things?" she sobs, her voice barely a whisper. "Zombies are only in the movies."

Jayne's concern is evident as she ponders this. "From what I could see on the phone before it broke, there was something about... um, sizzling rain? A space-storm or something."

Bettie shakes her head, her mind a jumble of possibilities. "I'm less worried about the how's and the why's than I am about the what's. I mean, if we knew what those *things* were, we at least stand a chance of beating them."

"Let's just call them zombies," Jayne says. "I've noticed something… they're all male. Have you seen any female… zombies?"

"No." It's a different voice, and it sends a jolt of terror through both women.

Bettie holds up her bottle, and Jayne grabs her camera, flash-finger at the ready.

"I come in peace."

As the young man emerges from behind the shower curtain, hands up, Bettie's heart races, unsure whether he's friend or foe. But as she takes in his normal eyes and handsome features, she realizes that she recognizes him.

"You're Marilyn's boyfriend," Jayne states, her voice tinged with relief. She lowers her camera.

"Who's Marilyn?" he asks, confusion clouding his expression.

Bettie and Jayne exchange a bewildered glance. If he's not Marilyn's boyfriend, then who is he? And more importantly, what does he know about the horrors that lurk beyond the bathroom door?

"The new girl," Bettie says. "Well, that's her stage name. We don't know what her real name is…" She just manages to catch herself from saying "was."

"Oh. I'm her brother, actually. Came here to pick her up after work and…" He shudders. "Where is she?"

Bettie and Jayne look at each other, then at him. Their bleak expression says it all. There's no point in trying to delay the truth of her fate.

"Welcome to our little sanctuary amidst the apocalypse," Bettie says with a bitter, humorless chuckle. "As for what's going on in here… Well, let's just say we've had our fair share of unexpected visitors tonight." She gestures towards the shattered window and the bloodstains on the floor, unable to suppress a shiver.

He slumps, then sits on the edge of the bathtub. "What's going on in here?"

"What's going on out there?" Bettie returns.

He pushes his hoodie down. "Well, first of all: Hi. I'm Jake."

"Hey. Bettie," she waves.

"I'm Jayne. So yeah, what's it like outside?"

"I wish I had a decent answer for you. Nobody knows. I woke up at two this morning to get my sister. The streets were jammed with people walking; odd for around here. Nobody driving, really, except for me. A few… weirdos. I knew something was off, but I didn't think much of it. It's L.A., y'know? So, I'm trying to listen to the radio, but nothing's coming in. Bunch of static. And it's pouring rain, but not steadily. Just in sudden bursts. The rain was a funny color, too. Then I thought I saw someone being attacked. Again—it's L.A.," he shrugs. "But I was getting worried, so I called my sister, but my phone was dead even though I'd just charged it. My headlights were flickering, too. My car died about three blocks from here. I had an umbrella, so I grabbed that and…"

"When did you get here?" Jayne interrupts.

"I dunno, like, an hour ago? At first, I couldn't get in. Then, some boomer in a beret came out and started threatening me. He left, and it was wide open when I got to the door again. Something just didn't look right to me. So I took a step back, and I walked around the corner. Then I saw these… men… or *things*, opening a window and trying to climb in. I ran back around to the door. I mean, Julie was in here, right? I had to find her. So I come in, careful. And I see these guys eating somebody. It was freaky, just like Fulci's classic *Zombi 2*."

Bettie perks up, and she feels her heart flutter. Good looking and knows his Italian horror? Too bad they're about to die.

Jake goes on. "There was nothing else I could do but try and ride it out and look for my sister. I was just about to do that when you came in. Now it's your turn: What's going on in here?"

"We know as much as you do," Bettie says. "I'm sure you heard what we said when we came in." She pauses, reflecting. "I'm sorry about Julie. We didn't know her before tonight, but she seemed cool."

"If it's any comfort at all," Jayne interjects, "they didn't eat her. They just… never mind. Seems like it was quick, though."

Jake takes a deep breath, as if setting aside the bad news to deal with later, looks around the room, his gaze stopping on Jayne's clawed cheek, and says, "Are you alright?"

Jayne gives him a wan smile. "Guys dig scars, right? I'll be fine."

He seems to accept her blithe lack of concern. "So, what's your plan?"

Bettie takes the reins. "Well, for starters, we need to find a way out of here," she says, her voice steady despite the rising sense of urgency. "I mean, duh. But it's not going to be easy. We've tried and let's just say it hasn't ended well. We started out as a group of four."

Jake nods, his expression grave as he considers their options. "Now you're back up to three. We'll stick together and watch each other's backs. And if we come across any more zombies, we'll need to be prepared to fight."

Bettie's resolve comes back as she braces herself for the challenges that lie ahead. "Alright then, let's do this. But first, does anyone have any ideas on how to deal with those zombies outside?

I mean, assuming we can get out the door, it's still not over."

As if on a cue of "action!" the knob to their left rattles. The door facing the dressing room begins to give way.

Jayne takes hold of her camera, ready to flash blinding light into the undead's eyes. Bettie, clutching her bottle like a seasoned warrior—or Nicolas Cage in *Leaving Las Vegas*—can't help but chuckle at the bizarre mise-en-scène. Meanwhile, Jake rips down the shower curtain with a dramatic flourish.

Bettie raises an eyebrow, questioning his unconventional choice of weapon. But before she can utter a single word, the bathroom door succumbs to the relentless pressure. With a thunderous crash, it swings open, and three grotesque, decaying creatures stagger into the room. Their guttural growls echo off the tiled walls, and the stench of their rotten flesh threatens to overwhelm them.

In a desperate attempt to blind them, Jayne clutches her camera and holds it high. She presses the button, and a dazzling flash of light illuminates the cramped space. But her plan backfires. One of the zombies, covering his eyes against the sudden burst of brightness, lunges at her with surprising agility. Its bony fingers close around the camera, yanking it from her grasp and causing her to cry out in pain and defeat.

Before Jayne can react, another zombie seizes the opportunity. It hurls itself at her, sinking its teeth into her shoulder. With a wrenching motion, it drags her through the doorway, and she disappears from view. The sounds of her struggle fade into the distance, and the remaining two monsters turn to follow the wounded prey.

"Jayne! Nooo!" Bettie's anguished cry echoes in the bathroom as her bottle slips from her grasp, shattering into a million shards.

In a courtly gesture, Jake spreads the shower curtain over the broken glass, shielding Bettie's feet. "We can't fight now, Bettie. We have to run," he says, his voice steady and reassuring.

Bettie can't help but think of her mother's words: "In movies, there's always a way out." She hopes with all her heart that her mom is right. With a heavy heart, Bettie nods. They'll mourn their losses and regroup later. But for now, they have to persist. And Bettie, channeling her inner action hero, is as ready for the challenge as she'll ever be.

Bettie's spike heels scrabble for purchase as she and Jake make a desperate dash for the back door, their footsteps echoing in the empty kitchen. The air is heavy with the stench of decay and fear, mingling with the scent of ancient cooking oil and mildew.

As they reach the Dutch door, which has a gaily curtained window on its upper half, Bettie reaches for the handle—then she sees yet another zombie lurking outside. Instead of turning the knob, she makes sure it's locked, then holds it steady.

The creature advances, its pale, fetid face soon pressed against the glass, its eyes devoid of humanity as it snarls menacingly and takes exaggerated sniffs. The curtains are sheer, offering no shield from its sinister stare.

Several jagged bolts of lightning dart across the backyard, their searing brightness in vivid contrast to the darkness. One particularly vicious bolt strikes a towering palm tree, and she watches in horrified fascination as it splits the tree in half. In an instant, flames erupt, casting an eerie, dancing glow that flickers ominously before the odd, colorful rain snuffs them out.

She trembles as she glances toward the shadowy figures shambling closer through the downpour. The zombies, relentless and unyielding, move with jerks and halts, their hollow eyes targeting the fragile sanctuary where Bettie and Jake take refuge. She swallows hard, feeling the weight of dread pressing down. The uncanny storm outside feels like a monstrous force, as if even the elements conspire against her.

She fears deep in her gut that if the relentless, ravenous undead don't tear them apart, it's only a matter of time before the lightning does. Each crackling flash is a deadly reminder of the horrors colliding outside, and she wonders just how long they can withstand the assault of both nature and the undead.

Bettie's heart thuds as she grips the door handle, holding it fast. The sheer force of her grip turns her knuckles white. She can feel Jake's hand close around hers, a steady and reassuring constant in the midst of this madness.

The creature beyond the door's glass pane has its decaying visage mashed against it, its vacant, milky-white eyes fixed unwaveringly on her.

"Dude, that goalie is pissed about something," Bettie remarks, her voice laced with dark humor that masks the distress bubbling beneath the surface. "I always knew my love for cheesy horror movies would come back to bite me in the ass, but I never imagined it would be quite so literal."

Jake lets out a low chuckle, his eyes never leaving the snarling zombie pressing against the window. "At least we'll go out in style," he replies, his tone matching Bettie's sardonic wit. He takes in her costume, complete with black stockings and fuck-me pumps. "Especially you."

Bettie can feel Jake's eyes on her, his gaze lingering on the way her skintight leopard wiggle dress hugs her hips and the swell of her push-up bra. Despite the dire circumstances, a small part of her thrills at the attention, a flicker of warmth igniting within her. She knows she must look a sight, her wig tousled and her makeup smudged, but somehow, she guesses she still manages to exude an air of that old black magic.

As they stand there, poised on the precipice of escape or doom, Bettie can't help but notice the way Jake's gaze travels down to her feet, taking in the sight of her spike heels. She silently curses the run in her stocking, a small imperfection in an otherwise flawless ensemble.

"Leave it to you to find the silver lining in a zombie invasion," she replies, her gaze darting around the kitchen in search of a potential escape route.

It's then that her eyes land on the staircase leading up to the third floor, a blip of optimism sparking within her. "Say, Jake," she begins, her voice taking on a conspiratorial tone, "what do you say we ditch this joint and make our grand escape through the crow's nest?"

He arches an eyebrow, his expression a mix of intrigue and skepticism. "The crow's nest? Isn't that a bit cliché, even for a cinema enthusiast like yourself? You have seen *Vertigo*, right?"

Bettie shrugs, her eyes dancing with a mix of dread and determination. "Cliché or not, it's our best shot at getting out of here alive," she retorts, already moving towards the staircase. "Besides, if we're going to die, I'd rather do it in a place with a killer view."

Jake shakes his head in amusement, his lips quirking into a lopsided grin as he follows Bettie's lead.

As she ascends the creaky stairs, she can't help but wonder if this is how it all ends—trapped at the top of a historic landmark, surrounded by the undead, with a handsome stranger by her side, and runs in her stockings. Bettie takes a deep breath, steeling herself for what's to come. She knows the odds are stacked against them, that the world outside is a terrifying and unknown landscape. But she also knows that they have no choice. They have to fight, to survive, to live to see another day.

They reach the top of the tight staircase, which has a squat, arch-topped door at its apex. She begins to count down, and her hand touches then tightens on the small brass door handle, ready to fling it open and face whatever frights await them. But even in the midst of this nightmare, she can't help but feel a flicker of something else, a spark of connection with the man beside her. And as they prepare to plunge into the unknown, Bettie finds herself clinging to that feeling, that small sequin shining in the darkness.

Chapter 18

The door is locked. "Womp, womp," Bettie says.

She gazes into the gloomy, cramped stairwell. This is far from an ideal situation. If they're cornered, there's no escape. Yet, they have no other option. She and Jake cautiously descend the stairs, making their way back into the kitchen.

The zombie that was at the door has vanished… perhaps now is the moment to vacate the house? They peek out the window, observing other monsters aimlessly wander around. Among them, she recognizes a few faces from the show but also spots a fast food worker and, surprisingly, a priest. *What an excellent day for an exorcism,* she thinks.

"The theater," she gasps, her voice strained with exertion. "We have to make it to the theater." If anything, they can turn on those overly bright, white-hot stage lights to keep the zombies away… assuming the iffy electricity stays on.

With one last glance at the back door, Bettie and Jake steel themselves for whatever's next. Together, they bolt from the kitchen, their footsteps echoing in the corridor as they race towards the faint whisper of hope that awaits them in the performance area.

The chairs have all been knocked around and toppled over, and the bar where Bettie had gotten a drink just hours before is a shambles. The once-sexy mixologist lays facedown in a pool of blood, with the server draped over her, also dead. Perhaps this isn't the best place to hide—but maybe these two didn't know about the zombies' aversion to light.

Bettie and Jake stop short when they see Footman onstage, stumbling around and armed with a high-heeled Lucite shoe, poised to strike. In the semi-darkness, he looks wild-eyed and desperate, his movements erratic and frantic. Bettie sees that his eyes are normal—or at least, she's pretty sure they are—but before she can say anything, Jake charges forward, ready to defend Bettie against what he believes to be another zombie threat.

"Heeere's Jakey!" he announces.

The fight that ensues is a chaotic flurry of limbs and adrenaline-fueled desperation. Jake swings crazily, his fists flying as he tries to subdue his opponent, who in turn lashes out with the spiked heel of the shoe, aiming for Jake's head.

Bettie watches in horror as the two men grapple on the stage, the sounds of their struggle rumbling through the empty theater. It's a clumsy, uncoordinated fight filled with desperate shoves, kicks, and punches.

"Get your hands off me, you damn dirty zombie!" Jake shouts.

"What?" Footman squeaks, his bow tie askew. "*You're* the zombie!"

Suddenly, Footman loses his balance and tumbles backward off the edge of the stage, his head connecting with a chair on the way down. Bettie winces at the squelching sound, the wet thunk of impact sending shivers.

As the client lies motionless on the floor, Bettie rushes to his side, her heart pounding with fear and guilt. She checks for signs of life and finds none.

"He was here earlier," Bettie murmurs, her voice trembling. "We called him Footman, because, well… Anyway…" *He's gonna be six feet under*, she thinks to herself—if he doesn't somehow come back to life.

Jake, still panting from the exertion of the fight, sinks down onto the edge of the stage, his hands quaking with adrenaline. "Are they all zombies?" he asks, his voice filled with uncertainty and dread.

Bettie joins him. "I guess so." She can't bear to tell Jake that she's pretty sure Footman hadn't been turned. Yet. Maybe it was only a matter of time. Who knew? Bettie gives her new friend a head-to-toe glance to see if he's been bitten or anything, but he looks fine.

Her head is hot, and she's sweating. She tugs at the bobby pins and pulls her wig off, revealing her golden blonde hair, just a few shades lighter than Jake's. She registers his glance of approval. She ruffles her damp locks, feeling much cooler and more comfortable—well, as comfortable as she can be under the circumstances.

"Seems to be connected to the storm," Jake says as if he just needs to say *something*.

Bettie nods. "It's like the opposite of *The Devil's Rain*. Oh, uh, *The Devil's Rain* is a movie—"

"B-horror starring William Shatner, Tom Skerritt, Ernest Borgnine, Eddie Albert, Ida Lupino, Keenan Wynn…" Jake says.

In unison, they conclude, "…And a young John Travolta."

They smile shyly at each other.

Jake brings his hands to his temples, thinking. "So in that movie, the monsters melted in the rain. In this case, it seems like the storm has… I dunno. A virus? Maybe it's like another Fukushima or something. A volcano? God knows what-all's been stewing underground for centuries."

Bettie can feel the burden of the situation pressing down on her, but she tries to push past the fear, focusing on finding a solution. Even in the midst of all this, she can't help but admire Jake's easy charm, which both comforts and unsettles her.

"Let's think this out. They don't like the light. That's for sure. But the light doesn't kill them, so they're not, like, vampires," Bettie muses aloud, her mind percolating with possibilities.

Jake lets out a nervous laugh. "This is the most ridiculous conversation ever."

Bettie nods in agreement, her brow furrowed with concern. "No shit. But we've got to figure this out."

"Well, if it's any consolation, it seems this thing only affects males," he offers, trying to lighten the mood.

"Great. Then they'll just kill me. Eyes or no eyes, you'll live on," she deadpans.

"Sounds peachy," Jake replies, his tone somber.

As the lights flicker and zap before finally going out altogether, Bettie feels truly hopeless. "Do you know anything about wiring?" she asks, grasping for any shred. "Maybe you can fix the lights."

Jake's flirty smile momentarily distracts Bettie from the dire situation they're in. "How sexist. Just because I'm a guy, you assume I'm handy," he teases. But his expression quickly turns serious as he considers her suggestion. "Maybe we could try tripping the breaker. You know where it is?"

Bettie shakes her head, her heart sinking as she realizes they're facing yet another obstacle. "No. We've never worked in this location before. And even if we had, I wouldn't know where it is."

"Alright. We'll have to do some reverse engineering. We'll have to look around and see where the power line comes into the building. Logically, the circuit breaker will be close to where the power comes in because it is easier and cheaper for the City's electricians," he says.

Bettie can't help but marvel at Jake's knowledge, even in the midst of chaos. Crazy. "How do you know that?"

Jake blushes. "I learned it when I auditioned to play Hot Electrician #3 on an episode of 'Reno 9-1-1.' I didn't get the part, though."

Oh, boy. Bettie thinks. *Not another actor.* Hollywood was full of them, and they were full of themselves. *Jake doesn't seem like that.* Then again, she doesn't really know him.

Her mind whirls through all the movies she's seen with electricity as a plot point… *Frankenstein, Shocker, Blackout.* Suddenly, she sees something—a shadow, a movement. Is it a monster? It's so dark! Guided by pure reflex, Bettie swiftly rolls down the snagged, diaphanous black stocking from her left leg, flings off her shoe, and coils the silky garment around her fists, prepared to stand her ground. She kicks off her remaining pump.

"What—?" Jake starts to ask, but Bettie silences him with a cautious gesture.

"Watch me, Jake," she whispers with a smirk, her voice colored with mock bravado, "you might just learn a thing or two about survival, and I'm not talking about your auditions."

Bettie's breath catches in her throat as she watches the shadowy figure stumble closer. Every nerve in her body tingles with adrenaline as she realizes the gravity of the situation.

It's not just a shadow—it's a zombie drawn by the scent of the living.

Chapter 19

Fear grips Bettie like the vice in *Casino*, but she refuses to let it paralyze her. With steely resolve, she takes a cautious step forward, her eyes locked on the intruder. The darkness seems to close in around her, amplifying the sound of Jake's barely-held breaths.

Time drags like the last two minutes of a bad movie as Bettie edges closer, the "weapon" in her hands suddenly ridiculous—she realizes that the stocking is about as threatening as a rubber chicken. Her inner monologue is live-tweeting a horror story: "Run, girl, run!" But she's got the stubborn focus of someone trying to thread a needle after three martinis. No backing down now. After all, it's not every day you're the underdog in a real-life zombie flick.

As Bettie sneaks up on the creature, its grotesque figure pops into high-definition. It lurches awkwardly, as if auditioning for "So You Think You Can Dance: Undead Edition" and failing miserably. She pushes her nausea aside, her mind laser-focused on the single goal: to neutralize the threat before it's too late. With a silent prayer on her lips, Bettie lunges forward, her makeshift garrote poised to strike.

Jake stares at her, dubious. "Everyone knows zombies can only be killed by a gunshot to the head. It's Romero 101."

Bettie catches the shuffling horror from behind, the stocking stretched tight between her fists. She wraps it around the creature's neck, the fabric taut. A glimpse of the ragged raincoat confirms her suspicions—it's The Flasher. He flails wildly, a grotesque dance of death, but her grip is unwavering, her arms fueled by adrenaline. She feels the stocking cutting through his soft, rotten flesh like a knife through butter. He stumbles, a marionette with its strings snipped, and collapses to the floor, each gasp a wet gurgle. With an unnerving jolt, Flasher regains his footing and, in an awkward, relentless pursuit of life, lurches into the murky shadows of the next room.

They watch him turn the corner and listen as he makes sloppy tracks into some unseen part of the old house. Then they hear him fall to the floor with a final gasp.

Bettie is proud of herself and wonders if Jake recognizes her moves. "Chuck Norris. *Force of One*, 1979!" Then she gives her new friend side-eye. "Thanks for the help, Jake."

"You sure don't need my help. You're all kinds of awesome."

She smiles, blushing. But there's no time to bask in the compliment. She puts her pumps back on and says, "Now, let's find that circuit breaker and get some light in here. I hate to say it, but I think we need to go back to the kitchen. When I was eye-to-eye with that zombie in the window of the Dutch door, I noticed some power lines behind him. Which means the kitchen is probably the spot. When I was a kid, I remember the fuse box was in our kitchen, and my mom hung a picture over it. Maybe there's something like that here…?"

Bettie and Jake navigate the dim, red-spattered hallway, their hands clasped tightly together. The atmosphere is thick with tension, and the distant rumble of more oncoming thunder adds to the never-ending sense of impending doom. The gaudy rain begins to pelt against the windows once again, sizzling and casting eerie, tinted shadows that dance along the walls.

As they sidestep the mangled cushions and smithereened chandeliers of the destroyed foyer, Bettie catches sight of Victor, his wooden face frozen in eternal surprise. Not that it looked any different, really—except for the missing eyes.

"Well, seems Victor won't be headlining any gigs soon," she comments dryly. She can't help but marvel at the absurdity of the situation—zombies attacking a ventriloquist's dummy?

Bettie's humor has always twirled on the edge of dark and light, a coping mechanism as finely tuned as her choreography. She knows Jake is in on the joke, creating a bizarre bond amid this madness. She might question his career choices, but in this horror show, she's glad for the company of someone who gets her.

As they tiptoe through the dimly lit hallway, the pair spot Whipping Boy in his garish Hawaiian shirt and khaki pants, clutching his riding crop as a makeshift weapon. With a creased brow and a comically exaggerated growl, he shuffles awkwardly among the zombies, hoping to pass unnoticed.

Bettie stifles a giggle at the incongruous sight. "Looks like Whipping Boy's taking his roleplaying a bit too seriously," she whispers to Jake.

Jake stifles a laugh, nodding in agreement. "Yeah, he's really committing to the whole 'undead' cosplay."

As the erstwhile patron successfully navigates through the room without drawing suspicion, he lets out a triumphant whoop and bolts off into another section of the house. The zombies, seemingly oblivious to his presence, continue their mindless shuffling, completely buying into his act.

Bettie shakes her head in disbelief, a look of approval gracing her face as she watches Whipping Boy's clever escape. "Well, I guess if there's one thing we've learned tonight, it's that you can't underestimate the power of a good costume and some enthusiastic growling." She wonders if maybe they should try mimicking the zombies themselves to get through the house undetected.

Glancing sidelong at Jake, she arches an eyebrow mischievously. "Hey, have you ever played a zombie?" she asks, the double meaning of her question not lost on her. Bettie can't help but admire Jake's handsome features, her mind wandering briefly to how he might look decked out in gory monster makeup. That's a movie she'd pay to see.

Jake chuckles, the sound rich and warm. He shakes his head, squeezing Bettie's hand reassuringly as they press on, determined to find the circuit breaker and restore some semblance of normalcy to their upside-down lives.

Bettie narrows her eyes, her grip tightening involuntarily as the shuffling groans of the undead grow louder around them. They seriously need to find that circuit breaker and restore power before they're torn apart by the ravenous horde.

Guided by fleeting memories of the evening's earlier calm, Bettie steers their hurried trek toward the kitchen. She sees gingham drapery skirting the far wall. The ghost of hope rises within her, a silent plea that behind that unassuming fabric lies their salvation. As they draw near, a wave of relief washes over them; the fuse box awaits just where she had envisioned.

"Here we go. Do you know what to do?" Bettie asks, her voice jumbled with optimism and apprehension.

Jake squints, scanning the array of switches and buttons. "In the movies, it's always some big lever. I don't see a lever."

"Me neither. Let's just push all the buttons. We can't be any worse off than we already are," Bettie suggests with a nervous chuckle.

"Yeah, maybe we'll just get electrocuted," Jake replies, his tone equally laced with dark humor.

As they ponder the fuse box, a strange phenomenon occurs—the sun outside breaks through the night at the speed of, well, light. It's an unnatural, uncanny sunrise, but it does the trick, casting a bright glow through the windows. All that's missing is fanfare music.

The sudden flood of sunlight blinds Bettie momentarily, a stark contrast to the gloom they've been navigating. She blinks away the dazzle, her eyes settling on Jake, who mirrors her bewilderment.

She hears the zombies screeching and scurrying in response to the sudden brightness, their movements reminding her of creepy crawlies fleeing from a switched-on room light. *Kind of like the cockroaches in my first apartment*—they were so big, they should have been paying rent.

"That's not normal, right?" Bettie asks, her voice low. The question is rhetorical—of course it's not normal. The sun doesn't just leapfrog into the sky like a stunt from a cheap special effects team.

Jake nods, his gaze still fixed on the window. "No way that's natural. The rain stopped too, like someone hit the pause button."

Bettie chews her bottom lip thoughtfully. It's too good to be true, this sudden reprieve from their night of horror. Her instincts scream at her to question everything—after all, in her preferred film genre, every silver lining usually has a cloud. "It feels like we're stuck in *The Beyond*," she muses aloud, half-expecting a dramatic twist to shatter their momentary relief. "Or maybe a slasher."

Jake rubs the back of his neck, his eyes scanning the room for any signs of danger. "Yeah, except those usually don't end with a deus ex machina sunrise. It's more... final girl standing amid carnage."

She snorts at his comment. "Final girl? I prefer leading lady, thank you very much."

They both fall silent for a moment, listening closely for any sign that the zombies have taken issue with the new daylight hours. Bettie can hear them—screeches and scuffles—but it seems distant now, scattered and in retreat.

"Is it safe yet?" Jake asks.

Bettie peers out the window cautiously. No sign of sizzling rain or shadowy figures. "I'm not sure if 'safe' is in our vocabulary right now," she replies. "But maybe this is our chance to make a break for it."

Jake meets her eyes, searching for an ounce of certainty.

Bettie wishes she could offer him some but finds herself coming up empty.

"I guess we don't really have a choice," he concedes.

She nods in agreement. Hopefully, they're no longer trapped in an unfolding shriek-fest that defies explanation—where every decision is life or death. She'd settle for a broken bone or two.

"Okay then," she says with resolve she doesn't quite feel. "Let's take our final bow and exit stage left while we can."

Chapter 20

Bettie and Jake tread cautiously from the kitchen into the gloomy, uncertain terrain of the blood-spattered hallway. The silence that envelops them is a chilling, unwelcome companion, its eerie sighs almost more unnerving than the guttural groans of the undead.

Their cautious steps lead them deeper into the passage, only to have their progress halted by the sight of a motionless body blocking their path. His vacant eyes, locked in an endless staring contest with the abyss, serve as an ominous reminder of the fate that awaits them should they falter. Bettie swallows a lump in her throat.

Her gaze lingers on the body, a sense of dismay washing over her. "Oh no," she murmurs, her voice a whisper. "It's The Richard." Despite the situation, she can't help but notice the man's impeccable coif, a testament to his vanity even in death. "At least his hair is still perfect," she notes with genuine admiration.

With a renewed sense of caution, Bettie and Jake continue their journey down the hallway. The air is rife with tension, their nerves on edge as they brace themselves for the next encounter.

Bettie's heart races as Kung Fu Zombie steps in front of them, a primal shriek escaping her lips as she instinctively flattens against the wall. Jake, too, presses himself against the cold surface, his breaths shallow and rapid.

Yet, the figure halting their progress isn't the fearsome adversary they anticipated. His motions are lethargic, devoid of the swiftness and savagery that characterized their foes. The terror that had seized Bettie's heart begins to ebb as she discerns a hint of the man he once was—the bashful spectator from the previous evening's cabaret who'd drawn the Queen of Hearts. His current state, however, betrays no recollection of the night's events. He appears dizzy and baffled, as if recovering from an overly indulgent bender.

When the beleaguered former Kung Fu Zombie diverts his path and trudges away, his bloodlust seemingly sapped, Bettie feels a blend of befuddlement and relief. "He's just... tired," she marvels, her voice a featherweight echo in the charged silence. Fatigue clings to her bones as well. The relentless ordeal is beginning to take its toll, each moment stretching her endurance thinner.

But their respite is short-lived as they spot The Flasher, disheveled but miraculously alive. The stocking, once wrapped around his neck, now hangs loosely, a curious accessory to his bewildered expression.

His gaze shifts towards the sunlight filtering through the windows, and Bettie can sense the puzzlement emanating from him. "What happened?" he asks.

Bettie studies him intently, her mind racing with questions and suspicions. Despite his disheveled appearance, there's something undeniably human about him in this moment—vulnerable and lost. With a tentative gesture, she reaches out to touch his arm.

Jake holds his breath, his eyes fixed on the scene unfolding before him.

To their relief, nothing happens. The Flasher remains unchanged, no signs of aggression or hostility. With a gentle tone, Bettie poses the question that lingers in the air, her voice tinged with empathy and curiosity. "You don't remember?"

He straightens, then looks confused, then indignant. "No, I don't." He cocks his head at Bettie. "Heyyyyy! Did you gals drug me?" The Flasher pats his clothing, locates his wallet and looks inside. The billfold is stuffed with cash. "Sorry," he mutters.

Suddenly, they hear a high-pitched shriek. This is a new sound.

Clenching Jake's arm like she was auditioning for the role of "Damsel in Peril: The Clingy Remix," Bettie's heels click a rapid morse code on the blood-slicked floor—SOS, and possibly, GTFO. Bettie can already taste the cliché 'fresh start' trope on her lips when a ghostly whisper cuts through their blockbuster escape.

The shrieking stops, and a faint female voice pierces through the veil of mystery. "Help me…"

Bettie stops cold. "Jayne? Jayne, is that you?"

The pinup's pulse plays hopscotch—her steps hitching, heels now drumming out an erratic beat of hesitation. She winces, her wit as reflexive as the need to survive, "Talk about your dramatic timing, Jayne."

The familiar strain of her friend's voice drapes a cold shroud over the flame of hope Bettie had been stoking. Glancing back toward the darkness they'd almost beaten, the sanctuary of daylight seems to dim. Once again, the reality of their situation had snatched the director's megaphone and was yelling, 'Cut!' on their not-so-triumphant exit scene.

"Maybe Julie's not dead!" Jake cries.

Jake's hopeful proclamation is met with Bettie's somber certainty. "No, Jake. She is," she says, her voice heavy with sorrow and resignation. The memory of Julie's lifeless, eyeless form is seared into her mind. "I fucking saw her."

Jake gestures to The Flasher. "You also killed a zombie right here."

The Flasher raises his eyebrows. "Huh?"

Jayne's desperate plea tugs at Bettie's heartstrings. With a resolute nod, she turns toward the source of the voice, her resolve unwavering despite the fear gnawing at her insides.

Bettie's stilettos clack against the sticky floor, a macabre metronome in the mausoleum-like quiet of The Fetish Factory. She can't help but compare the scenario to a scene right out of the slashers she loves, except she doesn't recall Jamie Lee Curtis ever having to navigate past pasties and G-strings in her escapades. *Fending off zombies in a glitter thong... Academy Award material right here.*

Despite the absurdity of her attire and the terror of the night, the image of Jayne trapped—possibly topping her last escaped assistant act—propels Bettie, one perilous, perilously high-heeled step at a time.

She steps inside the office, and she can't believe what she sees. The darkness and the sense of urgency had cloaked a lot last night, shielding her from the full horror. But now, in the unusually harsh light of morning, the true extent of the slaughter is laid bare before her eyes. It's too much... too ghastly, too overwhelming. Bettie feels her stomach churn as she takes in the grisly scene, fighting back the urge to retch. Despite her bravado and sarcasm, nothing could have prepared her for this nightmarish tableau of death and destruction.

Chapter 21

Irma's body is grotesquely positioned, half-draped over the leopard-print sofa, half-sprawled across the cluttered coffee table. Her eyes are torn out, one hanging from its meaty socket and the other missing. Her once smiling, wisecracking mouth is frozen in a silent scream. Her fingernails, polished silver to match her chic stage gown, are broken and torn, evidence that she fought for her life and lost.

Paul, back in his human form, sits beside her. He clutches Irma's lifeless hand, his face a picture of despair.

Jayne is perched on the floor behind them, her expression inscrutable, her eyes hooded in shadow. Bettie can only guess that she's dazed, shell-shocked by the night's horrors. At least she's alive.

Paul's gaze shifts to Bettie, his eyes glistening with unshed tears. "What happened?" he asks, his voice barely above a whisper. "Jayne says I killed Irma. I wouldn't do that."

Bettie finds herself at a loss for words. How can she possibly tell him that she witnessed him tearing into his better half's flesh alongside Gatekeeper, who was devouring her guts like they were sausages?

Just then, Jake joins Bettie, taking her hand in a silent show of support. The Flasher peeks into the room from the hallway but doesn't dare to step any closer.

Bettie trembles as she leans in towards Jake, muttering, "They really don't remember."

Jake, ever the pragmatist, scans their surroundings, his eyes settling on the glow of the lights. "The lights are on," he says, a hint of hope in his voice, "so does the phone work now?" He reaches into his front pocket, fingers fumbling for the familiar rectangular shape of his device.

Bettie, her mind still whirling from the revelation, shakes her head, a frown creasing her forehead. If he had the phone all along, why didn't he at least try it? Even if only to call his agent to plead for an escape from this awful audition for his life.

But their moment of contemplation is shattered as Irma springs back to animation with a guttural groan, her limbs jerking unnaturally. Simultaneously, white-eyed Jayne, her blonde hair matted and wild, jumps up with an unsettling agility, a low growl rumbling in her throat.

The sight of her friend transformed into this monstrous version of herself sends more than just a routine chill down Bettie's spine. She instinctively steps back.

Irma, her body now pulsing with an unnatural vigor that defies her years (not to mention her recent death), lunges at Paul with a ferocity that makes Bettie's heart lurch. The woman's hands, gnarled but viselike, wrap around his neck with a chilling swiftness. A gruesome crack reverberates around the space, bearing witness to the relentless power behind her assault. Bettie watches, her breath caught in her throat, as Irma sucks out Paul's eyes, a sickening spectacle that she wishes she could unsee. Blinking once, twice, Irma's own eyes are back in place—only they're green now, as Paul's had been, and staring blankly ahead, devoid of any warmth or humanity.

Bettie, Jake, and Flasher make a desperate, frantic dash for the front door. Their hopes of escape dangle precariously, a single misstep away from being shattered. But as they reach the end of the hallway, their path is blocked by an unexpected sight: Rosie and Marilyn, their once kind and inviting eyes now vacant and gleaming with an otherworldly, insatiable hunger—just like Irma, they had obviously taken eyes from victims which somehow replaced theirs but… it was just too much to think about right now.

"Seriously?!" Bettie exclaims, her disbelief mingling with panic. "We can't catch a break!"

Jake balls his hands into fists, his gaze ping-ponging between the ungainly duo in front of them like a spectator at a particularly slow tennis match. "Okay, it's go-time," he declares with the kind of boldness usually reserved for action heroes—or at least their stunt doubles.

Bettie huffs in agreement, planting her feet with readiness.

Just as they square up for an epic zombie boxing match, Whipping Boy catapults from the stairs to the ornate banister with all the grace of a drunken gazelle, his Hawaiian shirt flapping wildly, a symbolic "hang loose" gesture to the hideous girls. Bettie watches, torn between a scream and a cheer, as their unexpected knight in aloha print adds a slapstick element to their predicament.

Catching the absurdity of the moment like a hot potato, Bettie and Jake leap into the fray, feet pounding the grotty carpet like a backbeat to Whipping Boy's off-rhythm solo. As they synchronize with the human windmill of quirky heroism, Marilyn and Rosie's zombie two-step is no match for this impromptu jitterbug.

She sidesteps a withered limb, spiraling gracefully, and ducks beneath Rosie's reaching talon. Suddenly, Marilyn doubles down in the melee, and she finds herself entwined in a two-step with the slobbering shell. Jake is equally agile, his gaze flicking between foes while he parries their awkward onslaughts. Evading Marilyn's graceless dive with a nimble sidestep, his hand shoots out to brace her as she finds her balance—clearly, he's recognized his sister and can't bring himself to harm her. Meanwhile, The Flasher, his raincoat billowing around him, delivers a series of well-timed kicks and punches, his uncoordinated yet surprisingly effective moves keeping the undead assailants at bay.

Together, they form a formidable foursome, their determination to escape outweighing the odds stacked against them. With each strike and strategic maneuver, they inch closer to victory, their combined efforts gradually wearing down Marilyn and Rosie's feeble defenses.

Finally, with a triumphant shout, Whipping Boy delivers a decisive blow, sending Marilyn and Rosie staggering backward, their vacant eyes widening in surprise as they teeter on the brink of defeat, then fall flat on their derrieres.

Bettie grabs a broken spoke from the staircase just as Jayne and Irma shamble into the hallway. She casts a glance over her shoulder and her eyes meet Jayne's, who still sports that come hither sex kitten leer, though now it comes with a side of drool.

"Goodbye, darling," Bettie finds herself whispering. She tightens her grip on the jagged spindle in her hand and Jake gives her a nod, that kind of nod that says, "We got this," in a perfectly underplayed hero kind of way. As the undead divas lurch towards them, Bettie swings, adding a new meaning to "knock 'em dead." Despite the macabre makeover of her former pals, Bettie allows herself a brief second of melancholy for the bonds that once were.

With a primal roar, Whipping Boy charges forward, his riding crop swinging through the air with reckless abandon as he fends off the advancing zombies. Jake, his determination unwavering, follows suit, his fists clenched as he delivers a series of well-aimed blows.

Bettie herself joins the fray, her makeshift weapon swinging with precision as she ducks and weaves between Jayne and Irma's clumsy counterattacks. With each strike, she feels a surge of adrenaline, her focus honed on the singular goal of breaking free from their grasp.

And then, with a final push, they break through the ranks of their undead adversaries, bursting out onto the porch in a flurry of motion and determination. The morning sunlight washes over them, casting long shadows across the wooden planks beneath their feet. They lunge forward, intent on making a bee-line for the picket fence of salvation that borders the property.

With a defiant shout, Jake leaps off the porch. "I love you, Julie! …Sorry!"

The morning sun has the audacity to be chipper, pouring its ungodly cheerful rays all over Bettie as if she won the lotto rather than just barely escaping with her life. There they are, the lot of them, like the world's most mismatched cast. She lets herself simmer in the glow, pretending for a hot second that it's the spotlight after her killer final number rather than the opening act of *Who Knows What The Hell Is Next.*

Chapter 22

Bettie stands at the Mulholland Canyon lookout with Jake, the moon casting an eerie glow over the landscape below. It's been several days since they escaped the horrors of the zombie uprising. As she gazes out at the city that was once her happy home, Bettie wants to cry.

But she can't. She has work to do. She's been leaving evidence of their ordeal on smartphones scattered throughout the city, a desperate bid to document the madness that has consumed their lives. She holds one now, a phone she found lying on the ground beside a dented, abandoned Ferrari down the street.

"Somehow, we got out of there," Bettie murmurs. "The girls... they were weak, just waking up. Or maybe they let us go." She pauses, her mind drifting back to that fateful night. "We lost track of The Flasher and Whipping Boy. Jake and me... we stayed together."

Jake's smile provides a fleeting moment of warmth before he redirects his attention to the enigmatic expanse below them. The celestial orb above seems to loom larger than ever, a bloated witness to the unthinkable chaos that has gripped their world.

The persistent unease that Bettie harbors refuses to subside, the notion that their respite from peril might be only temporary. "It didn't take us long to piece together that there was some kind of *Ladyhawke* thing going on," she remarks to the future listener of her message. "You know the film, right? A tragic romance riddled with a curse where the lovers are eternally separated by their shifting forms—one a hawk by daylight, the other a wolf come nightfall." A mirthless chuckle bubbles from her lips. "Except in our twisted version, the infected shift in a deadly dance of day and night... male zombies hunting under the cloak of darkness, females prowling in daylight."

Her voice dwindles, lost in the stark truth of their plight. "They keep returning, reanimated over and over... and our numbers are dwindling. Somehow, Jake and I have dodged the virus's touch. For now..."

She collects herself and goes on to describe some inexplicable anomalies, such as the fact that newer cars equipped with computers won't run, but cell phones still work—as long as you don't try to communicate. You can't make phone calls, send texts, leave comments, or write emails, but you can browse the web… with plenty of glitches, making the effort just barely worthwhile.

Bettie's words dissolve into the silence, her eyes locked on the moon-swept vista. The uncertainty of what lies ahead is palpable, yet she's steeled herself for the trials that await. What else can she do? She refuses to give up or give in.

Bettie's mind wanders back through the blur of the past days and nights. They've taken refuge in mansions that dot the Hollywood hills, opulent homes now deserted, their owners either fled or fallen victim to the calamity that has seized the city.

In one of these houses, she'd joked to Jake as they raided a walk-in pantry, "Who knew the zombie apocalypse would have such great snacks?"

Jake had grinned back, popping open a can of gourmet peaches. "Yeah, beats fighting over a can of Soylent Green."

After that, they raided the owner's closet, where they found an array of suits, red ties, and even a clear raincoat. Jake couldn't resist trying on the classic ensemble.

Bettie appraised him, hands on her hips. "Very Patrick Bateman, circa 1987."

"Thanks," Jake replied, turning like a model. "I call it stabby chic."

The dwellings were their only source of sustenance—not to mention umbrellas to protect them from the rancid rain as well as the sun's sinister rays. Unlike the male zombies, who couldn't bear light, daytime's undead divas had no problem with it—they weren't fond of water, though.

The couple had found soft beds, changes of clothes, running water, and soap… but they didn't want to get too comfortable. As they moved from one mansion to the next, they met other survivors, haggard faces peering out from behind fortified gates. But there was an unspoken agreement between Bettie and Jake to keep it just the two of them; a duo against the dystopia. It seemed safer that way—fewer chances for betrayal, or worse, attachment in a world where every sunrise or sunset could be your last.

Bettie took an odd pleasure in the eerie tranquility that enveloped these houses at night. She'd certainly never be able to afford to live in one of these places otherwise. But the once-manicured gardens were slowly withering under the oddly hued rain that seemed to poison rather than nourish. It was a double feature—from *Invasion of the Body Snatchers* to something out of *The Day of The Triffids*—only instead of killer plants, they had ruinous rain.

The electricity was a lasting casualty, too. Streetlights flickered and died like the final breaths of a dying star. During their first night in a particularly grand manor with a home theater, she'd attempted to enjoy a B movie classic, but halfway through, the screen sputtered and went dark. Even her most trusted companion had failed her. Of course, she knew how it ended.

Or did she?

Their connection to the outside world was sporadic at best. The news breaks they managed to catch were fragmented, often in languages neither she nor Jake understood. They still hadn't determined whether the rain virus was confined to their area.

"And here I thought L.A. traffic was as bad as it gets," she mused while scanning for any broadcast in English. When static answered her again, she tossed aside the battery-operated radio with a dramatic flourish fit for *Sunset Boulevard*'s finest.

Jake caught it before it hit the floor. "We'll find something eventually," he said with cautious optimism.

"Yeah," Bettie replied, her tone heavy as she looked out through dirt-streaked windows at a sky that seemed to bleed into twilight. "We're definitely living the dream."

Bettie shivers as a gust of wind snakes its way through the canyon, carrying with it the musty scent of desolation. She wraps her arms around herself, feeling the chill of the evening penetrate her pilfered leather jacket. The city below sprawls out like a dormant ogre, its streets once pumping with life now silent. Even the birds and bugs seem to have flown the coop.

Beside her, Jake shifts his weight from one foot to the other. "We should keep moving," he says, his voice low, eyes scanning the horizon for any sign of movement.

She nods, her thoughts lingering on their dwindling supplies. They'd been lucky so far, scavenging what they could from the vacant homes of Hollywood's elite. But even those provisions have limits, and they have to keep going—a moving target is hard to scent.

* * *

At sunrise, the merciless new heat is beating down on them. Bettie's lungs burn, but the grit coursing through her veins propels her to keep moving.

Suddenly, a cacophony of snarls and guttural cries erupts from behind them, the shuffling footsteps of pursuers drawing ever closer. Bettie risks a glance over her shoulder, her stomach lurching at the sight of the pack of female zombies closing in, their ragged forms contorted in mindless hunger.

"This way!" Jake shouts, veering towards a sleek, vintage sports car parked on the curb.

Bettie's gaze snaps to the vehicle, her heart leaping with hope as she spots the glint of a keychain dangling from the visor. They might just make it out of this particular hellish situation.

As they near the vehicle, a lone male zombie lurches into view, its decaying face twisted into a distorted snarl. Bettie curses under her breath, wondering how there's a him among the hers. But all she can focus on now is keeping the creatures at bay. Her grip tightens around the metal pipe she wields as a crude weapon, and she lets go of the rolling suitcase that contains their few worldly possessions.

"I'll handle this one!" she calls out to Jake, who's already fumbling with the keys.

The zombie lunges at her, his gnashing teeth snapping mere inches from her face. Bettie deftly sidesteps the attack, swinging her pipe with all her might. The solid metal connects with the creature's skull with a sickening crunch, sending it staggering backward.

"Eat a bowl of fuck!" Bettie jeers.

But the brief victory is short-lived as the pack of female zombies descends upon them, their collective moans and shrieks piercing the air. She whirls around, her pipe raised in a defensive stance, her heart pounding in her ears.

"Hurry, Jake!" she cries, fending off the onslaught of grasping hands and snapping jaws.

The engine roars to life, and Jake throws open the passenger door. "Get in!"

Bettie doesn't need to be told twice. She grabs the suitcase and darts towards the car, batting away an undead monster that lunges at her. With a burst of adrenaline-fueled strength, she shoves the creature back, sending it crashing to the cement.

She leaps into the passenger seat, suitcase in her lap, slamming the door shut behind her just as Jake peels away from the curb. The tires squeal in protest, and Bettie twists in her seat to watch the horde fade into the distance, their anguished cries ringing in the sweltering afternoon air.

"Holy shit," she sighs, "I was beginning to feel like I'd just jumped onto Flight 180." She brings a fist to her lips and imitates a loudspeaker, "And your *Final Destination*, ladies and gentlemen, is *Zombieland.*"

They don't get far before the car runs out of gas… that's the problem with the new, horrifically sunny days—it dries up not only water but gasoline as well.

They're in the Los Feliz area now, not too far from Bettie's apartment. But far enough. They break into the nearest empty home and hole up for a few hours. Their treks are aimless, and they never seem to get far from the heart of Hollywood. It's as if they're being contained by an unseen forcefield. Or maybe they're both just helplessly lost without GPS.

The couple venture out finally, and as they walk down the hillside, Bettie's eyes catch a flicker of light from one of the houses below. Her heart skips a beat—other survivors? Or something sinister?

"We need to check it out," she says to Jake, nodding toward the light.

He hesitates for a moment before nodding back. They proceed with caution, weaving between the cover of trees and overgrown hedges.

They reach the home, and Bettie peers through a gap in the fence. A once extravagant pool is now half-filled with murky water and debris.

Jake reaches for the gate latch but Bettie grabs his arm. "Wait." Her voice is firm. "We don't know what we're walking into."

He nods and they both watch in silence as another figure joins the first inside the house.

Bettie has a plan—they'll circle around to the front and try to get a better look through one of the windows before making their presence known. It's risky, but it beats charging in blind.

With careful steps that barely rustle the fallen, dead leaves beneath their feet, they make their way around to the front of the house, ready for whatever or whoever awaits them inside. The first thing Bettie notices—and it's impossible to miss—is the pink, high-heeled shoe above the door. The neon doesn't flash, but it's definitely the same beacon she knows well.

She points at it, and Jake shrugs.

"Thieves?" he whispers.

Bettie takes a deep breath, steeling herself. She glances at Jake again, who gives her a nod of encouragement. She raps her knuckles against the glossy painted wood. "Shave and a haircut, two bits," she mumbles under her breath, a wry smile playing at the corners of her mouth.

The door creaks open, revealing a familiar face—none other than Irma Wacl, emcee extraordinaire and co-owner of The Fetish Factory. But this Irma is different. Her eyes are clear, and her skin is free of the telltale signs of zombie infection.

"Well, well, if it isn't Morticia Addams," Bettie quips, her voice laced with a mix of relief and suspicion.

Irma's lips curve into a knowing smile. "I see your snark hasn't been dulled by the apocalypse, Betts."

The pinup points up at the neon sign. "And I see you brought a piece of home with you," she remarks.

Irma nods, her expression grave. She steps aside, inviting them in with a sweep of her hand. Bettie and Jake exchange a glance before crossing the threshold, their senses on high alert.

"We knew it would catch your attention. Paul and I... we've been following you," she says. "You've been sort of, well, herded in this direction."

Bettie's eyebrows shoot up. "Stalking during the end of days? That's a new one."

But her sarcasm falters as they enter the next room. There, restrained in a chair, is Paul—or what's left of him. His skin is mottled and gray, his eyes blank.

Irma sighs, her shoulders sagging under the weight of their shared burden. "We've been... trading places."

Bettie tells Irma that she and Jake, whom she reveals is Marilyn's brother, figured out that plot twist early on. "A real *Freaky Friday* situation, minus the laughs."

Irma shakes her head. "If only it were that simple. When we're human, we remember nothing of our time as zombies. And when we're zombies..." She trails off, her gaze drifting to Paul's restrained form. "We're too far gone to be of any use. It's only in these moments, just before dusk and just before dawn, that we have some semblance of clarity. It doesn't last, though."

"I'm assuming you didn't invite us over for tea and crumpets," Bettie remarks, looking around the house and wondering what happened to its previous occupants... she assumes they were dispatched by either Irma or Paul.

Irma's expression hardens with determination. "We need to find a cure for this virus. And for that, we need help from the uninfected. From people like you and Jake."

Bettie exchanges a glance with her beau, a silent agreement passing between them. They're in this together, for better or worse.

"Alright, Irma," Bettie says, her voice steady despite the dread gnawing at her. "Where do we start?"

Chapter 23

Paul blinks, trying to clear the fog from his mind. The last thing he remembers is locking himself in the bathroom, terrified of what Irma might do in her zombie state. Now, he finds himself in the living room, surrounded by Bettie, Jake, and a restrained Irma.

"What's going on?" he asks, his voice hoarse. "Why am I out here? And why is Irma tied up?"

Bettie steps forward. "Paul, we need to talk. Irma told us that you're a zombie too, but only at night. Is that true?"

Paul shakes his head, confusion clouding his features. "What? No, that's impossible. I'm not a zombie. I'm just trying to keep Irma safe and not get killed by those... those *things* out there."

Jake exchanges a glance with Bettie before asking, "But Paul, don't you remember anything about being a zombie yourself? Irma said—"

"Irma's not in her right mind," Paul interrupts, his voice rising. "She's been like this ever since the rain started. I've been doing my best to keep her from hurting herself or anyone else."

Bettie kneels beside Paul, placing a hand on his shoulder. "Paulie, we want to help you both. But we need to know what's really going on. Can you tell us anything about the creatures or how this all started?"

Paul runs a hand through his sandy, graying hair, his eyes distant. "It was the rain. Something in the rain changed people. Irma was one of the first to turn. I've been trying to find a way to cure her, to bring her back, but..." His voice cracks, and he looks away.

Bettie squeezes his shoulder, her voice gentle. "We'll figure this out together, Paul. You're not alone anymore."

As Paul nods, a glimmer of faith in his eyes, Jake moves to check on Irma, ensuring her restraints are secure. They settle in, determined to unravel the mystery of the zombie-inducing rain, and find a way to save Irma and the others affected by this strange disaster.

Paul leans back in his chair, his mind reeling from the revelations. Bettie and Jake, one a stranger he'd only just met, have become his unlikely allies in unraveling the mystery behind the outbreak.

As the trio delves deeper into their shared experiences, an hour slips away unnoticed. Bettie, Jake, and Paul, each with their unique perspectives, relay the pandemonium that has engulfed their world. Paul, despite the gnawing anxiety for Irma, finds solace in the camaraderie, his too-cool-to-care beatnik persona forgotten.

Eventually, the weight of their discussions begins to take its toll. Bettie suggests a break, a chance to let their minds breathe. She playfully enquires about any old movies, clarifying with a chuckle that she's not in the mood for stag films.

Paul, also a connoisseur of classic cinema, obliges with a knowing smile. He gets a large suitcase, then rummages through a stack of old VHS tapes, finally selecting one with a worn-out cover. With a practiced hand, he hooks up an ancient VCR to a mini generator, then to their unwitting host's TV set.

The hum of the machine is a comforting reminder of simpler times. As the opening credits roll, Jake and Paul sink deeper into their seats, their eyes heavy with fatigue. Bettie, however, remains alert, her gaze glued to the flatscreen as if drawn by an unseen force.

"Wait, go back," Bettie says, pointing at the TV screen. "Did you see that?"

Paul rewinds the tape, and they watch as a grainy image of a UFO hovers over a small town, its inhabitants stumbling through the streets like mindless drones.

"That's just like what's happening here," Paul murmurs, leaning forward in his seat. "But that's scripted, right? It can't be real."

Bettie shakes her head, her eyes wide with realization. "But what if it is? What if the rain virus is something that's happened before, and these old movies are trying to warn us?"

As they continue to watch, Paul notices a pattern emerging. The zombie outbreak is preceded by strange weather phenomena and unusual electromagnetic readings. He reaches for a stack of papers on the coffee table, flipping through the rainfall data he'd collected over the past week.

"Look at this," he says, pointing to a series of spikes in the data. "These anomalies in the weather patterns, they match up with the electromagnetic surges we've been seeing. What if they're connected?"

Jake leans in. "You think the rain virus might be extraterrestrial in origin? Like some kind of deliberate attack?"

Paul nods, his mind pinging with possibilities. "It's the only thing that makes sense. The way the sickness spreads, the way it affects people... it's not like anything we've seen before. And yet, those movies…"

As they sit in silence, each wandering in their own thoughts, Paul feels a weight lifting from his shoulders. For the first time since the epidemic began, he doesn't feel alone in his fight to save Irma. With Bettie and Jake by his side, he knows they'll stop at nothing to uncover the truth and find a way to restore her and the others affected by the virus.

Paul's reflections race with the implications of their discovery. If the zombie outbreak is indeed the result of extraterrestrial experimentation, then what does that mean for humanity? Have they been nothing more than lab mice, their lives and memories subject to the whims of an alien intelligence?

He glances at Bettie, seeing the dread in her eyes. "I don't want to forget," she whispers, her voice trembling. "Jake, my friends, memories of my mom... they're all I have left."

Paul reaches out, placing a comforting hand on her shoulder. "I know," he says softly.

Jake shakes his head, his jaw set with determination. "We can't let this virus win. We have to find a way to stop it, no matter what it takes."

As they sit watching the rest of the movie, Paul can't help but wonder what the future holds. Will they be able to uncover the truth, or will they become just another petri dish in the aliens' twisted experiment? Whatever, Paul knows one thing for certain: they can't give up. Too many lives are at stake.

He takes a deep breath, pushing aside his fears and doubts. "Okay," he says, his voice steady. "Let's get to work. We need to figure out how to track these surges, see if we can pinpoint the source of the virus."

As they hunker down over the rainfall data and talk sci-fi film plots, Paul feels a flicker of hope ignite in his psyche. They may be just three people against an unknown menace, but they have something the aliens don't: the strength of the human spirit and the unwavering mission to protect the ones they love.

Paul watches as Bettie paces the room, her eyes alight with excitement. She gestures animatedly, her voice rising with each word.

"Okay, hear me out," she says, turning to face Paul and Jake. "In *The Day the Earth Stood Still*, they used a makeshift satellite dish to communicate with the alien ship. What if we did the same thing?"

Paul raises an eyebrow, intrigued by the idea. "You think we could intercept their transmissions?"

Bettie nods. "Exactly! We just need to find the right materials and build a dish big enough to pick up their signals."

She gets online and goes straight to IMSDb.com, pulling up a copy of the *Close Encounters of the Third Kind* screenplay. Flipping through the PDF pages, she points to a diagram of the iconic Devil's Tower.

"See this? They used a similar concept in the movie, using the mountain as a natural amplifier for the alien transmissions. We could do the same thing but with a satellite dish instead."

Paul leans in, studying the diagram closely. His mind zips ahead, already envisioning the components they'll need to make Bettie's idea a reality.

"It could work," he says slowly. "But we'll need to find a way to decode the transmissions once we intercept them."

Bettie's eyes sparkle with mischief. "Leave that to me. I've got a few tricks up my sleeve."

None of them are covert aerospace engineers or anything, but they each have some knowledge of the inner workings of machinery and electronics. Bettie was often tasked with fixing the forever temperamental cappuccino machines at the diner where she'd worked; Jake made cash on the side as a Geek Squad guy; and Paul knew how to fix all the old cars in his and Irma's fleet.

As they commence the task of gathering materials and sketching out plans, Paul can't help but be in awe of Bettie's ingenuity. She's more than just the proverbial pretty face. Her love for movies and geekdom has provided her with a unique perspective on their predicament. He steals a glance at Jake, who is already elbow-deep in a pile of scrap metal and wiring, his forehead creased in concentration. Together, the three of them make a formidable team, each one bringing their own strengths and expertise to the table.

As time ticks by, they continue to work tirelessly, fueled by a potent mix of determination and countless cups of coffee. Paul feels a renewed sense of purpose coursing through his veins. With Bettie's plan, they might just have a chance to unravel the mystery behind the zombie outbreak and put an end to the alien threat that looms over them.

As the last beams of sunlight begin to fade from the windows, Bettie and Jake exchange a somber glance. They approach Paul, who has already come to terms with the reality of his situation. He has even taken the time to scribble a note to himself in the hopes that the next time he regains his humanity, he will remember enough to keep the plan moving forward. Reluctantly, they secure him, ensuring that he poses no threat to them when the zombie instincts take over.

Chapter 24

The moment the sun rises again, they get to work. Bettie's fingers—more nimble now that she's removed her acrylic nails—dance across the control panel, connecting wires and adjusting settings with a fierce determination. Sweat beads her brow, but she doesn't pause to wipe it. Every second counts.

Jake hunches over a tangle of cables, his brow furrowed in concentration. "I think this goes here..." He twists two wires together, and a spark flashes. "Damn it!" He yanks his hand back, shaking it.

"Careful, kid." Paul's voice is gruff but not unkind. He leans in, squinting at Jake's work. "Here, let me."

As Paul takes over, Bettie steps back, surveying their progress. The satellite dish is starting to take shape, a Frankenstein's monster of scavenged parts and improvised solutions. It's not pretty, but it might just work.

A low moan drifts through the window and Bettie tenses. The zombies are getting closer. She glances at the door, half-expecting to see rotting hands clawing at the barricades.

"We need to hurry," she says, her voice tight.

Jake nods, his jaw clenched. "I'm doing my best."

"Your best might not be good enough." Paul's words are blunt, but there's no malice in them. Just a grim acknowledgment of the stakes they're facing.

Bettie takes a breath, forcing herself to focus. She can't let fear get the best of her. Not now. Not when they're so close.

She turns back to the control panel, her fingers flying across the buttons. "Almost there," she mutters. "Just a few more adjustments..."

The dish hums to life, the sound almost drowned out by the snarls of the approaching killers. Bettie's pulse quickens, but she doesn't let herself hesitate.

"That's it!" Jake whoops, pumping his fist in the air. "We did it!"

Paul nods. "Not bad, kid. Not bad at all."

But their triumph is short-lived. A crash echoes from downstairs, followed by the splintering of wood. The creatures have broken through.

Bettie meets Jake's eyes, seeing her own fear reflected back at her. But beneath the fear, there's something else. Something fierce and unyielding.

Determination.

Bettie's heart flip-flops as the zombies shuffle in, their ravenous wails filling the air. Each thud and scrape sends a shiver down her spine, a visceral reminder of the nightmare that's still closing in on them. She recognizes Dolly Danger, Panama Red, and Josephine.

She glances at Jake, seeing the same fear furrowed on his face—his eyes wide, lips pressed into a thin line. They're trapped, with nowhere to run. The walls seem to close in on them, the once secure room now feeling like a coffin. Bettie swallows hard, her mind racing for a plan, any plan, to get them out of this alive.

But Paul has an idea. "Irma," he whispers, his voice urgent. "She can control them."

Bettie stares at him, incredulous. "Are you insane? She's one of them now!"

Paul shakes his head, a glint of determination in his eyes. "She was always in command of you girls. If anyone can get through to them, it's her."

Bettie watches, her breath wedged in her throat, as Paul approaches Irma. The zombie strains against her bonds, her teeth gnashing. Paul leans in close from behind, his lips brushing against her ear as he whispers something Bettie can't hear.

Then, with a swift motion, he unties her.

Bettie's blood runs cold. This is it. They're done for. Irma will turn on them, and they'll be torn apart by the very woman who once told bad jokes for a living.

But Irma doesn't attack. Instead, she rises to her feet, her movements stiff and jerky. She turns towards the front door, where the other zombies are still clawing and snarling.

And then, miraculously, they fall silent.

Bettie watches in amazement as Irma shambles forward, her steps growing more confident with each passing second. The others part before her, their heads bowed in submission.

Irma reaches the door and wrenches what's left of it open, sunlight spilling into the room. Bettie squints against the sudden brightness, her eyes watering.

And then, one by one, the zombies follow Irma outside. They move in a single file line, their movements synchronized and precise. It's as if they're under a spell, compelled to obey their former leader.

Bettie can hardly believe what she's seeing. She glances at Paul, who has a small, satisfied smile on his face.

"I told you," he says softly, eyes slick with unshed tears. "She always was in command."

Bettie watches as Irma leads the dancers outside, their movements spookily synchronized. She can hardly believe it worked, but there's no time to dwell on the miracle. They have a satellite to finish.

She turns back to the control panel, her fingers fumbling over the buttons and dials. Jake and Paul work beside her, their faces tense with concentration. The clock is ticking, and they know it.

Paul glances out the window, squinting at the setting sun. "We've got an hour, tops," he says, his voice gruff. "If we don't get this thing working before nightfall..."

He doesn't finish the sentence, but he doesn't need to. They all know what's at stake. If they fail, Paul will revert back to his zombie form, and their chances of survival will plummet with yet another night closing in.

Bettie tries to steady her nerves. She can't afford to let fear cloud her judgment. Not now, when they're so close.

"Almost there," Jake mutters, squinting. "Just a few more adjustments..."

The apparatus hums to life, the sound filling the room. Bettie holds her breath, hardly daring to hope. Could it really be working?

They step back, staring at the device with a mix of awe and trepidation. The seconds tick by, each one feeling like a mini eternity.

And then, suddenly, the air crackles with static. Bettie listens as a series of cryptic signals begin to emerge from the speakers. The sounds are unlike anything she's ever heard before, a strange mix of clicks, whirrs, and pulsing tones.

She exchanges a glance with Jake, seeing her own astonishment reflected in his eyes. "Is that...?"

"Alien communication," Paul breathes, his voice hushed with reverence. "It has to be."

Bettie stares at the satellite, hardly daring to believe it. After all this time, all this struggle, could they really have made contact? Could this sloppily constructed saucer be the key to saving humanity from the zombie plague?

The signals continue, growing stronger and more complex with each passing moment. Bettie strains to make sense of them, but they're unlike any language she's ever encountered. So much for the tricks she promised.

All she can do now is listen and hope that somehow, someway, they'll find a way to decipher the message. Because if they can't, then all of this will have been for nothing.

Chapter 25

Bettie stares at the satellite intently, as if she's reading the subtitles for a Guy Ritchie movie. The signals continue to pour from the speakers, a cacophony of strange clicks and whirrs that make no sense to her human ears.

"Okay, so we've made contact," she says, her voice dripping with sarcasm. "But unless one of you is fluent in Martian, I don't see how we're going to translate this."

Jake scratches his head, looking perplexed. "Maybe we could try running it through a language algorithm? Google translate? Or—"

Suddenly, the signals change. The clicks and whirrs fade away, replaced by a series of strangely familiar phrases.

"E.T. phone home," a mechanical voice intones.

Bettie's jaw drops. "Is that...?"

"From the movie," Paul breathes, his eyes wide with wonder.

The voice continues, cycling through a series of movie quotes that Bettie recognizes instantly. "Klaatu barada nikto," it says, followed by "Live long and prosper" and "May the force be with you."

Despite the gravity of the situation, Bettie can't stifle her laughter. "Seriously? The aliens are communicating with us through movie quotes?"

Jake looks relieved. "Hey, at least it's a language we understand. And they must know that."

As the trio listens, the quotes begin to form a pattern. It's as if the aliens are trying to tell them something, using the grammar of cinema as a bridge between their two cultures.

And then, with a sudden clarity that takes Bettie's breath away, the message becomes clear.

"The rain," she whispers, her voice trembling. "It *was* them. They did this to us."

Paul nods, his face wan. "Just as we thought. But why? A test," he says. "To see how we would react in the face of a global catastrophe."

Bettie feels a surge of anger rising in her gorge. All this suffering, all this death, and for what? So some intergalactic civilization could study them?

But even as she fumes, she can't help but marvel at the absurdity of it all. Here they are, three survivors in a world gone mad, decoding an alien message through memorable movie lines. It's like something out of a B sci-fi flick. Only this time, the stakes are all too real.

Bettie chuckles to herself as she ponders the bizarre gender dynamics at play in this alien-induced apocalypse. In a world where the rain virus has flipped traditional roles on their head, she finds herself equal parts bemused and perplexed.

"You know, it's kind of funny," she says, her voice dripping with cynicism. "All these years, society's been telling us that women are the weaker sex. But now, with this virus, it's 50/50."

"At least we now know why we're seeing a mix sometimes… it goes strictly by biology," Jake surmises. "Which, I think, means even if some of the zombies are transgendered, the aliens are only able to mess with their DNA, not their hearts and minds."

Bettie nods, still deep in thought. Even amidst an apocalyptic scenario, she reflects, outdated notions about gender still had a way of creeping into the conversation. The true enemy was the rain virus itself, not those afflicted by it. Now more than ever, they need to band together to turn the tide.

As she mulls over the space invaders' form of communication, a sudden idea strikes her. "Hey," she says, her eyes lighting up with an impish glint. "What if we give these aliens what they really want?"

Jake and Paul both turn to her, their expressions quizzical.

"Think about it," Bettie continues, her voice growing more animated by the second. "They're communicating with us through movie quotes. They're studying us like some kind of cosmic reality show. So why not give them the ultimate Hollywood experience?" She beams, her mind already brimming with possibilities. "We could write a screenplay just for them. Cast ourselves in the starring roles. Give them the fame and attention they so clearly crave."

Jake's eyes widen, a slow smile spreading across his face. "You know, that's not a bad idea."

Paul nods, stroking his stubbled chin thoughtfully. "It could work," he muses. "But we'd have to make it good. Something that really showcases the best of humanity."

Bettie laughs, her eyes sparkling with mirth. "Oh, I think we can manage that. After all, we've got a burlesque dancer, an actor, and a pinup wrangler on our team. If anyone can put on a show, it's us."

And just like that, the seeds of a plan begin to take root. It's a long shot, Bettie knows, but in a world where the impossible has become the everyday, she figures they might as well give it a try. And if there's one thing Bettie's learned from a lifetime of watching movies, it's that sometimes, the craziest ideas are the ones that just might save the day.

* * *

Bettie sashays into the room, her golden hair bouncing with each step. "Time to tie up the old man for the night. Can't have him going all zombie on us again, can we?"

Jake grabs some rope from the counter. "I never thought I'd be into bondage, but here we are." He smirks at Bettie.

She rolls her eyes. "Save it for the bedroom, blondie."

Together, they secure Paul to a chair, his head lolling to the side as the virus begins to flow through his veins once more. Bettie pats his cheek. "Sleep tight, don't let the aliens bite."

A knock at the door makes them jump. Jake peers through the peephole. "It's Irma."

"Well, let her in; don't leave a lady waiting!" Bettie places a hand on her hip.

Irma enters, uncertainty etched on her face. "What in the world is going on? I feel like I've been in a fog all day."

"That's because you were a zombie, sweetie." Bettie shrugs. "It happens."

Jake fills Irma in on the situation with the aliens and their twisted game of Trivial Pursuit. "And Paul here is our secret weapon. When he's not trying to eat our eyeballs, that is."

Irma shakes her head in disbelief. "This is all too much. I need a drink."

"Don't we all," Bettie mutters. She'd noticed an expensive bottle of champagne in the fridge earlier, but its gold foil and celebratory artwork seemed to be mocking her, so she let it be.

With Paul secured and Irma filled in, exhaustion finally catches up with them.

Bettie yawns widely. "I don't know about you, but I'm ready to crash. Being fabulous is tiring work."

Jake nods in agreement. "Let's hit the hay. We'll need our rest if we're going to beat those alien bastards at their own game tomorrow."

Bettie slinks off to bed, the shuffle of her slippers fading down the hall. Jake takes one last look at Paul, still slumped and secured in the chair, before turning out the light.

She slips under the covers, her body aching from the day's exertions. Sleepy-eyed, she watches as Jake shucks his clothes and slides in beside her, his warmth instantly comforting. She nestles into his arms, feeling safe and protected.

"I'm glad you're here with me," she whispers, tracing circles on his chest. "I don't think I could do this alone."

He kisses the top of her head. "I'm not going anywhere. We're in this together."

She takes a deep breath. "My real name is Elizabeth. Elizabeth Carey."

"Elizabeth," Jake repeats, savoring the sound. "It's beautiful. But you'll always be my Bettie."

Tears prick at the corners of her eyes. In this moment, despite the danger surrounding them, she has no doubt that Jake is her soulmate—or at least her leading man for a three-picture deal.

They might have a future together if they can just survive this Irwin Allen-scale disaster. Exhaustion quickly pulls them under.

In her dreams, Bettie sees her mother, radiant and healthy, the way she looked before the cancer ravaged her body. Her mom smiles at her, a knowing look in her eyes, and Bettie feels a sense of peace flow over her. Somehow, she knows her mother is guiding her, watching over her from beyond. The dream shifts, and Belinda Joy's face morphs into that of Bettie Page. The iconic pinup queen of yore winks at her, a rascal's grin on her rosy lips. In that instant, Bettie realizes that the legendary beauty is more than just her namesake—she's her guardian angel, a source of strength and inspiration.

With renewed determination, she sleeps on, ready to face whatever challenges the dawn may bring.

Chapter 26

Bettie's eyes snap open as the first rays of sunlight peek through the window. She sits up with a groan, her body aching. Glancing over at Jake, who is still snoring softly, she reaches out and shakes his shoulder.

"Rise and shine, sleeping beauty," she says. "We've got work to do."

Jake mumbles something unintelligible and rolls over, but Bettie is persistent. She yanks the covers off him and he yelps, sitting up with a start.

"What the hell, Bettie?" he grumbles, rubbing his eyes.

"No time for beauty sleep, Jake. We've got a screenplay to write and scenes to shoot."

Bettie's gaze wanders around the bedroom, taking in the faded floral wallpaper and the framed family photos on the dresser. A half-burned vanilla candle sits on the nightstand, its scent long gone. She wonders about the people who once called this place home. Did they make it out alive? Or are they stumbling around out there, their minds gone, their bodies rotting?

She walks over to the window, peering out through the crack in the curtains. The street below is empty, save for a few abandoned cars and the occasional piece of trash blowing in the scorching wind.

Bettie turns back to Jake, who's still sitting on the bed, looking lost. She feels a pang of sympathy for him. He didn't ask for any of this. None of them did.

"Hey," she says softly, sitting down beside him. "I know this sucks, but we're lucky to have a roof over our heads. And each other."

Jake nods, a small smile tugging at the corners of his mouth. "Yeah, I guess you're right. Though I could do without the zombies. And aliens."

"You and me both," Bettie chuckles, bumping her shoulder against his. "But hey, at least we've got plenty of material for our screenplay."

Jake gives a soft chuckle, shaking his head. "Yeah, who knows? If we survive this, Hollywood will be lining up to make movies about a bunch of misfits fighting the undead in a fetish club."

"Hey, stranger things have happened," Bettie says, feeling a little lighter despite the circumstances. "I mean, look at *Sharknado*."

Together, they make their way downstairs to where Irma is tied up, thrashing against her restraints. Paul is slumped in the corner, looking haggard but human once more.

Bettie approaches him cautiously. "Paul? You with us?"

Bettie eyes him warily, not entirely convinced that he's back to his old self. She takes a cautious step forward, studying his face for any signs of the monster within.

"You really don't remember anything?" she asks, her eyes narrowed.

Paul shakes his head, looking frustrated. "It's all a blur. I know I'm... different at night. And Irma..." He glances over at his counterpart, still thrashing against her restraints, her eyes wild, white, and unseeing.

"She's a zombie during the day," Bettie confirms, her tone matter-of-fact. "And you're one at night. But right now, we need you to focus. We've got a plan to save the world, and we need your help. It'll come back to you. Let's get you some coffee, okay?"

Jake steps forward, holding out a hand to help Paul to his feet. "We're going to write a screenplay," he explains, his eyes gleaming with excitement. "And then we're going to film it. If we can get this thing out there, we can warn the rest of the world. Maybe we can stop this thing before it spreads any further."

Paul looks skeptical, his eyes darting between Bettie and Jake. "A screenplay? How is that going to help?"

Bettie holds up a pen and a stack of paper. "Think about it, Paul. You've been in the entertainment industry for years. You know how powerful a message can be when it's delivered through a story. If we can create something compelling enough, something that really resonates with people—I mean, aliens—maybe we can make a difference."

For the next hour, they huddle together, brainstorming ideas and scribbling furiously. Bettie's hand cramps but she pushes through, determined to get this thing done.

The crew then transforms the eerie house into their makeshift movie set. No room is left unutilized, and no prop is overlooked. From the dusty attic to the dank basement, they commandeer every nook and cranny, repurposing furniture and knickknacks with inventive flair. Just as they're putting the finishing touches on the place, a loud crash booms from downstairs. Bettie's head snaps up, her heart pounding.

"What was that?" Jake whispers.

Bettie swallows hard. "I think our leading ladies have arrived."

They've been expecting this, bracing themselves for the moment when the zombies come looking for fresh blood and new eyeballs to munch on. But it gets worse.

The sight that awaits them is like something out of a nightmare—one that's a real gut-punch. Jake's sister lurches towards them, her eyes dull and opaque, her white halter dress a bloodstained rag. Tristan, who used to rule the stage with her stunning figure and captivating presence, is now a pathetic parody of herself. Rosie and Jayne, girls

Bettie has shared countless laughs and tears with backstage, are nearly unrecognizable, their bodies contorted into unnatural positions as they stumble forward. The sight of her friends and colleagues reduced once again to shambling, lifeless husks of their former selves makes Bettie want to cry all over again.

Beside her, she can feel Jake trembling, his breathing shallow and rapid. She glances over at him, seeing the anguish fixed across his handsome features as he stares at what used to be his sister. "Julie...?" His voice cracks, barely above a whisper.

But there is no recognition in Marilyn's lifeless gaze, no flicker of the warm, shy girl she once was. She reaches out with grasping, clawing fingers, her luxurious hair now knotted and filthy, hanging in stringy clumps around her livid face.

Bettie's chest tightens with sorrow for Jake, for the unimaginable pain he must be feeling. She wants nothing more than to wrap her arms around him, to offer some small measure of comfort. But there's no time for that now. They have a job to do, a mission to complete, if they want any chance of making it out of this hellscape.

She risks a glance at Irma, bile rising in her throat at the deranged glee in the older woman's irisless eyes as she watches the scene unfold. Irma strains against her bonds, her body wracked with spasms and twitches, the hunger for violence and destruction radiating off her in palpable waves. *Just you wait,* Bettie thinks to herself. *Welcome to primetime, bitch.*

Squaring her shoulders, Bettie turns to face Jake and Paul, determination etched into every line of her face. "Alright, boys," she says, forcing a note of her trademark sass into her voice. "It's showtime." She does jazz hands. "Let's give these zombies their final bow."

But even as the words leave her lips, a spark of inspiration ignites in Bettie's mind. She turns to her companions. "That's it!" she exclaims, snapping her fingers. "We'll muzzle these suckers and use them as more than just extras in our little film. It'll be the most realistic zombie flick ever made!"

Jake looks at her like she's reenacting *The Thing With Two Heads.* "Uh, Bettie... you sure that's wise? I mean, they're still flesh-eating monsters, even if they used to be our... uh, family."

But Bettie is already elbow-deep in a nearby supply closet, rummaging around until she emerges with an armful of leather belts, dog leashes, rubber balls, and rolled-up pairs of socks. "Oh ye of little faith," she jokes, flashing him a cheeky look. "Trust me, sugar. We'll have 'em trussed up tighter than Eli Roth's *Thanksgiving* turkey. No biting, no problem!"

It takes some doing (and more than a few close calls), but eventually, they manage to wrangle Marilyn, Tristan, Rosie, and Jayne into makeshift muzzles. Paul takes charge like the seasoned pro he is, barking out orders and directing the snarling, drooling zombies into position.

Bettie has to admit, it's pretty damn impressive. This crazy scheme of hers just might work after all... "Alright, places, everyone!" she calls out through cupped hands.

She grabs the script, her keen eyes scanning over the pages like Stanley Kubrick after the fiftieth take. She's determined to ensure they hit all the crucial story beats, not letting a single detail slip through the cracks. It's not exactly the studio production she's always dreamed of, but damn if they aren't going to give it their all.

Bettie settles into her role as she watches the unfolding scene before her. The zombies, once her dear friends and colleagues, now serve as macabre thespians, their snarls and groans adding an unsettling authenticity to the film.

As Jake uses an iPhone camera set to twenty-four fps to shoot from his own POV, Bettie can't help but admire his dedication. Despite the horror of seeing his sister reduced to a mindless marionette, he pours his heart into every line, every gesture. She feels a swell of pride, knowing that together, they just might pull off this whacky production.

But even as the thought crosses her mind, a sudden commotion erupts from the corner of the room. Bettie whirls around, her heart leaping into her throat as she sees Irma, her muzzle hanging loosely around her neck, lunging towards the nearest zombie with a feral growl.

"Irma, no!" Bettie screams, dropping the script and rushing forward. But it's too late. Irma's teeth sink into Rosie's flesh, tearing and ripping with savage ferocity.

Chaos erupts as the other monsters, sensing the fresh blood, strain against their restraints. Bettie's mind races, desperately searching for a way to contain the situation before it spirals out of control. The once-docile extras suddenly find themselves on the receiving end of Irma's insatiable appetite for the spotlight... and flesh. They tear at their gags, desperate for release. But the alpha is relentless, her strength fueled by an insatiable hunger for violence and destruction.

Jake and Paul spring into action, grabbing whatever weapons they can find. Bettie's breath comes in sharp gasps as she watches the scene unfold, her heart pounding in her ears. She knows they're outnumbered, outmatched, and rapidly running out of options.

As Irma turns her bloodshot eyes towards her, a chilling smile spreading across her gore-streaked face, Bettie feels a shiver of pure terror

sprint down her spine. She braces herself, fearing
that the real fight of her life is about to begin...

Chapter 27

"Oh, for the love of Margo Channing!" Bettie exclaims, her voice dripping with exasperation. "Leave it to Irma to steal the scene, even in death."

As the other zombies recoil from Irma's attack, Bettie's gaze darts around the room, searching for a way to bring the unruly starlet back in line. Her eyes land on a discarded leg stocking, and a wicked grin sweeps across her face.

"Time for an encore of my greatest hit," she quips, snatching up the stocking and stalking towards Irma with determined strides.

Irma, caught up in her own performance, barely has time to register Bettie's approach before the stocking is looped around her neck and pulled taut. Bettie's muscles strain as she wrangles the thrashing zombie, her years of burlesque dancing proving surprisingly useful in subduing the unruly dead.

"Alright, Miss Thing," Bettie grunts, tightening her grip on the stocking. "That's enough of your scene-stealing antics. We've got a movie to make, and you're not going to ruin it with your diva demands."

Irma chokes, coughs out a few chunks of curdled blood, then raises her gnarled hands in surrender.

With the zombie successfully muzzled once more, Bettie turns back to the rest of the group, a triumphant smirk playing at the corners of her mouth. "Now, where were we?" she asks, brushing a stray lock of hair from her face.

As filming resumes, Bettie can't help but feel a sense of déjà vu wash over her. Thinking back to the cramped quarters of the old Queen Anne house, the flickering lights, the snarls and groans of the undead... it's all too familiar, a twisted echo of that fateful night at The Fetish Factory.

But this time, Bettie is determined to rewrite the ending. With limited resources and a ragtag crew of survivors, they painstakingly recreate the scenes that have haunted their nightmares, pouring their blood, sweat, and tears into every frame. The film is shaping up to be a quirky sci-fi comedy, recounting the wild and terrifying events of the past few days from the humans' perspective. As surreal as it feels, there's a strange catharsis in turning their trauma into art.

It's not Hollywood, Bettie muses wryly, but it's a hell of a lot better than being zombie chow. If they survive this, maybe their little film will become a cult classic—an ode to the resilience of the human spirit in the face of unimaginable horror. And if not, well... at least they'll go out with a bang and a punchline.

As the sun begins to dip lower in the sky, Bettie feels a sense of urgency wash over her. They are racing against the clock now, desperate to finish shooting before they lose the light. She rallies the troops, urging everyone to stay focused and work as efficiently as possible. This film is their lifeline, their one shot at getting the truth out there. Failure simply isn't an option.

As the final scene wraps, Bettie rushes to edit the video on Jake's phone, her pulse pounding with a mixture of excitement and trepidation. She knows that time is of the essence and every second counts. Her fingers fly over the screen as she patches their masterpiece together, carefully selecting the most impactful shots and weaving them into a compelling narrative. Bettie's mind races as she works, hoping against hope that their message will be received and understood by not only the rest of the world but also the aliens above. She pours every ounce of her creativity and passion into the edit, determined to make it the best it can possibly be.

With just moments to spare before the sun dips below the horizon, Bettie hits the final button and holds her breath as the film is transmitted via satellite to the waiting extraterrestrials. Thank goodness for that—the aliens may have cut off their communication with fellow humans, but not to them.

She closes her eyes for a second, sending up a silent prayer that their efforts will not be in vain. This is their one shot, their last chance to save humanity from the infected hordes.

She leans back in an easy chair, exhausted but satisfied. "That's a wrap, folks," she says with a sigh. "Let's just hope those space suckers have a sense of humor."

The minutes tick by, each one feeling like forever and a day.

Suddenly, a strange, metallic soundwave fills the air, seeming to emanate from somewhere above. She rushes to the window, her eyes wide with fear and curiosity. As she peers outside, her jaw drops in disbelief.

There, just in front of the house, hovers a classic silver spaceship. It's like something straight out of an atomic-era drive-in movie, all sleek lines and gleaming metal. The saucer hangs suspended in the air, just a few feet off the ground, its presence both awe-inspiring and terrifying.

Bettie's mind reels as she tries to process what she's seeing. Could this really be happening? Are the aliens actually here, responding to their film? Or is this some kind of elaborate hallucination, a byproduct of the stress and trauma of the past few days?

Before she can even begin to formulate an answer, an insistent dinging sound cuts through her thoughts. She glances down at the phone in her hand, frowning in confusion. The screen lights up with an incoming message, but the number is unlike anything she's ever seen before—a string of strange symbols and glyphs that shift and change before her eyes.

With trembling fingers, Bettie taps the screen to open the message. Her heart gallops as she reads the words that appear. The message is short and cryptic, but its implications are staggering.

"We have received your transmission," it reads. "Prepare for contact."

Bettie's breath hitches as she looks back out the window at the waiting saucer. This is it, she realizes. The moment of truth.

"Alright, you space weirdos," she mutters under her breath. "Let's do this."

The screen crackles to life with an image, and someone appears—the alien king, his expression unreadable.

Bettie stares at the screen, her heart pounding as the leader's face comes into focus. But it's not a single, cohesive visage that greets her—instead, it's a dizzying collage of famous actors from throughout cinema history, morphing and shifting like a kaleidoscope of celluloid dreams… the only thing missing is their eyes.

One moment, she sees the haunting countenance of Rudolph Valentino, smoldering with silent film intensity. The next, it's the chiseled jaw of Cary Grant, the epitome of old Hollywood magnetism. Marlon Brando's brooding brow gives way to James Dean's rebel sneer, while Rita Hayworth's sultry pout dissolves into Grace Kelly's timeless poise.

The effect is both mesmerizing and unsettling, a surreal patchwork of familiar faces that seem to embody the very essence of the movies Bettie loves so much. She can't help but feel a sense of awe at the sight, even as a shiver shimmies down her spine.

It's clear that the alien leader is drawing upon the collective cultural memory of Earth's cinema, using these celebrated visages as a way to communicate with the humans below. But what message is he trying to convey? Is it a sign of respect for their art form, or a subtle manipulation designed to put them at ease before they move in for the coup de gras?

Bettie leans forward, studying the ever-shifting face with a blend of fascination and unease. She knows that this moment is crucial—the fate of humanity hangs in the balance, and every word, every gesture, could be the difference between deliverance and destruction.

As the seconds tick by, Bettie finds herself holding her breath, waiting for the extraterrestrial to speak. The anticipation is almost unbearable, a knot of tension coiling tighter and tighter in her gut. She glances over at Jake, seeing her own anxiety mirrored in his eyes.

Finally, the alien leader's mouth opens, and Bettie braces herself for whatever revelation is about to come. The air seems to crackle with electricity as the first words begin to form, and Bettie knows that the fate of the world hangs on every syllable.

"You had me at hello," he intones, his voice a perfect imitation of Renée Zellweger in *Jerry Maguire*. A facsimile of Renée's face appears, then vanishes, replaced by yet another Hollywood star.

Bettie exchanges a glance with Jake and Paul.

"I'm sorry, what?" she asks.

"Life finds a way," the alien replies, this time channeling Jeff Goldblum in *Jurassic Park*.

Paul steps forward, his brows knitted. "Are you... still quoting random movies at us? What did you think of *our* movie?"

The alien gives a single nod. "I see dead people," he says, looking like Haley Joel Osment in *The Sixth Sense*.

"Oh, shit," Bettie whispers. "Does he mean us? He's gonna kill us? Zap us on the spot? If he didn't like the movie, all he had to do was hit the 'thumbs down' icon."

Jake grips her hand. He's trembling.

Bettie lets go and throws up her hands in exasperation. "Did you watch our film or not?"

The king's expression softens as he continues to churn through various personas. "I'm not bad, I'm just drawn that way," he says, quoting Jessica Rabbit from *Who Framed Roger Rabbit.*

"…And?" Bettie prompts.

The extraterrestrial continues to shapeshift, then settles on a smooth, featureless, genderless face. It's quiet. Finally, a hint of a mouth appears, and the being spouts a line from the screenplay Bettie had poured her heart and soul into crafting. Her eyes widen in disbelief at hearing her own written words echoed back by this otherworldly being.

Jake's eyes widen. "Wait, is that… is that from our screenplay?"

Bettie takes his hand again and squeezes, blinking back tears of joy.

The alien nods. "We have watched your film and it has moved us deeply. We understand now the beauty and resilience of the human spirit. We cannot in good conscience continue with our plan to destroy your planet."

Bettie feels a wave of relief pour over her. But could it really be that simple? "So what happens now?" she asks.

"The greatest trick the devil ever pulled was convincing the world he did not exist. And like that… he is gone," the alien says, in a spot-on

Verbal Kint impression. And with that, the screen goes black.

Bettie turns to Jake and Paul. "Kevin *Spacey…* well, that was on-brand!"

The existential weight of the air lifts, they hear a great upward WHOOSH! from outside, and then birdsong. Everything feels different. It feels right.

"I can't believe it actually worked," Jake marvels. "We just saved the world with a no-budget zom-com." He laughs and pulls her into a hug. "You're a genius, Bettie. An absolute genius."

Paul nods in agreement. "I never thought I'd say this, but I'm proud to be a part of the human race today." He reaches into his back pocket and pulls out his rumpled beret. He smooths it and puts it on in a gesture to the return of normalcy.

Bettie looks around at the remnants of their makeshift movie set, feeling a profound sense of accomplishment and pride. Against all odds, they had done the impossible—they had outsmarted the technologically advanced aliens and saved the entire world from destruction. And all it took was a little creativity, a lot of determination, a healthy dose of movie magic, and the ability to think outside the box.

She turns to Jake and Paul with a triumphant expression and takes a breath. But before she can speak, a sudden commotion coming from the outside catches their attention.

There's a deafening crash of thunder, followed by a torrential downpour that pounds against the roof like a thousand drumming fists. *Oh, fuck… not again*, Bettie thinks. Lightning strikes so close to the house that the blinding flash makes her jump, casting shadows of their silhouettes that flicker like specters across the walls. The windows flare with a searing brilliance reminiscent of an atomic bomb test, throwing the room into stark relief. It's worryingly quiet for a moment, then Bettie hears the tentative chirp of a bird. What does it mean?

Chapter 28

Bettie rushes to investigate, her heart pounding with a jumble of anticipation and trepidation. As she tentatively cracks open the front door, she stops dead in her tracks, her eyes widening in disbelief at the sight before her.

The zombies are in the front yard—Irma, Tristan, Jayne, Rosie, and Jake's sister, Julie—and they're in the throes of a miraculous transformation. Their once-decaying flesh begins to knit back together, the sickly pallor of death replaced by the warm glow of life. Their eyes, previously milky and vacant, now sparkle with renewed vitality and awareness.

Bettie watches in awe as Irma blinks in confusion, her hand flying to her throat as if searching for the phantom stocking that had once restrained her. Tristan and Jayne exchange bewildered glances, their movements no longer jerky and uncoordinated but fluid and graceful. Rosie lets out a joyful laugh, twirling around in a giddy circle as she marvels at her restored body. And Julie falls into her brother's arms, tears of relief streaming down her face as they embrace.

Bettie's gaze shifts to Paul, who stands off to the side, watching the scene unfold with a mixture of wonder and apprehension. But as the moments tick by and no signs of infection or decay appear, it becomes clear that he, too, has been spared from the zombie virus.

Tears sting at the corners of Bettie's eyes as she watches the former zombies reunite with their loved ones, their laughter and sobs of joy filling the air. She knows that the road ahead will not be easy—there is still so much to rebuild and heal from—but for now, in this moment, all that matters is that they are alive and together.

Bettie surveys the scene, taking in the surreal scene of their ragtag group of survivors—human and formerly undead alike—all huddled together in the aftermath of their harrowing ordeal. "Well, looks like we've got ourselves a real-life *Breakfast Club* here, minus the angsty teen drama and plus a whole lot more flesh-eating."

Jake rolls his eyes but can't hide his smile. "Only you'd find the humor in a zombie apocalypse, babe."

"Hey, if we can't laugh at the absurdity of it all, then what's the point?" Bettie retorts, her eyes twinkling with mischief. "Besides, I think we've earned a little levity after the hell we've been through. It's not every day you get to save the world with a horror flick and a motley crew of mangled misfits."

She opens the door, and ushers the women inside. She looks around at their unlikely group of allies—the former zombies still marveling at their transformation, Paul with his beatnik swagger, and of course, Jake, her partner in crime and love. "You know, if this were a movie, we'd be the plucky underdogs that nobody believed in, but who managed to beat the odds and come out on top. Cue the triumphant eighties power ballad and the slow-motion victory walk."

Irma, ever the diva, strikes a pose and declares, "Darling, I was born for the slow-motion victory walk. And the power ballad, for that matter!"

Bettie can't help but laugh at that, feeling a surge of affection for these people who have become her family. "Alright, alright, let's not get ahead of ourselves. We still have a lot of work to do to rebuild and make sure this whole *Devil's Rain* thing never happens again. But for now, I say we celebrate our win."

She goes into the kitchen to get that big bottle of champagne from the icebox. Jake follows and pulls Bettie into a passionate embrace, holding her like it's the first time—not like it might be the last. Their lips meld in a scorching kiss, sending waves of desire coursing through her. It's like he's trying to imprint every inch of his essence onto her, and she finds herself lost in the moment. Her senses quiver, but their moment is interrupted by the rest of the crew.

"That was amazing, you two," Paul, always the director, says with a chuckle. "Let's do it one more time, just to be sure."

Bettie and Jake glance at each other, their eyes saying everything that needs to be said. They're ready to give it their all, again and again, until they get it just right—later when they're alone in her apartment.

Bettie throws her arm around Jake's shoulders and raises the bottle in a toast. "To the weirdest, wildest, most dysfunctional group of heroes this side of a John Hughes movie. May we always be ready with a quip, a kick, and a killer screenplay when the world needs saving."

Irma gets some glasses, and everyone joins in the toast, passing the bottle around, their laughter ringing out through the room.

Bettie gazes out the window, her eyes widening as she spots a couple approaching the house. They look confused and disheveled, their clothes dirty and torn, but they are undeniably human. She rushes to open the door. "I take it this is your place?" she asks, unable to contain her excitement.

The men exchange a bewildered glance, clearly taken aback by the scene before them. "Uh, yeah," one of them replies hesitantly. "What's going on here?"

Bettie beams, practically bouncing on the balls of her feet. "Hey, guess what? We saved humanity!" she announces, her voice ringing with triumph.

The couple's eyes widen in uniform disbelief, but Bettie ushers them inside before they can ask any more questions. They join the group, still trying to process the surreal scene before them.

As Bettie goes in for another toast, one of the homeowners suddenly notices the bottle in her hand. "Hey," he says, his brow furrowing. "That was my best bottle of bubbly."

Bettie freezes, smiling coyly. "Oops," she says, handing the magnum back to him. "Sorry about that. We got a little carried away with the celebrations."

The man takes the bottle, but he can't help but smile at the absurdity of the situation. "It's okay," he says, shaking his head in amusement. "I guess saving the world earns you a drink or two of the good stuff."

Bettie clinks her glass against his. "Damn straight," she says. "And trust me, you're gonna want to hear the whole story. It's a doozy."

As the group settles in, Bettie begins to regale the newcomers with the tale of their unlikely victory, her voice animated and her gestures grand. The couple listens in rapt attention, their initial disbelief giving way to awe as the story unfolds. "But it's even better when you see it! It's right here on Jake's phone."

He pulls the device from his back pocket and holds it up. "I've got wi-fi again," he announces, then starts scrolling. He looks confused. "Our movie… it's gone."

Bettie shrugs, then shakes her head in amazement. She figures the aliens took it with them. It doesn't matter.

Who would have thought that her love of campy horror movies and her quick wit would one day save the human race? It's almost too incredible to believe. But the proof is right here in front of her—in the expressions of relief and joy on Jake and Paul's faces, in the silence where the alien's threatening transmissions used to be.

They did it. They actually did it.

Index of Quotes
(several are paraphrased)

"Dude, that goalie was pissed about something." *Freddy Vs. Jason*, 2003

"E.T. phone home," *E.T.: The Extra-Terrestrial*, 1982

"Eat a bowl of fuck!" *Night of the Demons*, 1988

"For God's sake, girls, get out!" *The Amityville Horror*, 1979

"Get your hands off me, you damn dirty zombie!" *Planet of the Apes*, 1968

"Heeere's Jakey!" *The Shining*, 1980

"Help me…" *The Fly*, 1958

"Hold still, Ralphie, or I'll shoot your eye out!" *A Christmas Story*, 1983

"I'm no angel." *I'm No Angel*, 1933

"I see dead people." *The Sixth Sense*, 1999

"I'm not bad, I'm just drawn that way." *Who Framed Roger Rabbit?* 1988

"Is it safe yet?" *Marathon Man*, 1976

"It's showtime." *All That Jazz*, 1979

"Klaatu barada nikto." *The Day the Earth Stood Still*, 1951

"Let's buzzzz!" *Slumber Party Massacre 2*, 1987

"Life finds a way." *Jurassic Park*, 1993

"Live long and prosper." *Star Trek: The Motion Picture*, 1979

"May the force be with you." *Star Wars*, 1977

"The boy can't help it." *The Girl Can't Help It*, 1956

"The greatest trick the devil ever pulled was convincing the world he did not exist. And like that... he is gone." *The Usual Suspects*, 1995

"We come in peace." *The Day the Earth Stood Still*, 1951

"We're not in Kansas anymore." *The Wizard of Oz*, 1939

"Welcome to hell, motherfuckers!" *Tales From the Hood*, 1995

"Welcome to primetime, bitch." *A Nightmare on Elm Street: Dream Warriors*, 1987

"What an excellent day for an exorcism." *The Exorcist*, 1973

"You had me at hello." *Jerry Maguire*, 1996

Afterword

I hope you've enjoyed this novelization and expansion of 2017's *Cabaret of the Dead* (aka *Fetish Factory*), my first feature film as a writer-director. (I must thank Jennifer and Michael Biehn, and Lony Ruhmann for giving me my break!)

Fortunately, working as an entertainment reporter and film critic in la-la-land for most of my life helped prepare me for the wild ride. That, and a love of old-school drive-in movies, ala the late, great Roger Corman… because we sure didn't have the budget of the big boys in Hollywood!

Time was also a luxury we could not afford. In my three-day writing blaze of the first draft of the script, *Cabaret of the Dead* took on a strong comedic element, plus old-school burlesque was added to the mix to help pass the time before the zombies showed up.

Once we found the perfect location and cast the leads, everything else shambled into place. We shot the film in five days (the usual production schedule for a low-budget film is two weeks to eighteen days), and it was a nonstop adventure!

Anyone who knows Los Angeles real estate is aware that vintage charmers are often razed to make way for the shiny and new. We lucked out in a major way finding a location through one of our actresses.

I'd originally written the script tailored around a live theater setting—because our story takes place when the burlesque ladies are giving a performance, and—"what?!"—the zombie apocalypse strikes. Hate when that happens. But what we got was even better: An 1800s Queen Anne/Victorian mashup that's not only actually used for burlesque shows, but is aching with atmosphere. This place is like the architectural love child of *The Amityville Horror* house and *Bordello of Blood*. Perfection!

Okay… maybe not completely perfect. I'd written several "haunted hallway" scenes into the script, but there is only one hallway in the actual house. All right… *half* a hallway. But we made lemonade out of arterial blood: since the movie is so campy, the fact that the characters keep returning to the tiny, zombie-infested corridor only adds to the intentional absurdity. It's all very *Scooby-Doo*!

What's more, the "Horace P. Dibble House" is recognized as Historical Monument #157 on the California Landmark list, and miraculously, as far as I've been able to glean, *Cabaret of the Dead* is the only movie ever shot there. The rather conspicuous house has an interesting backstory all its own, having been named after a notorious murderer who killed a man with a knife in 1896. Perhaps that is why our zombies were having so much fun.

Speaking of fun, the movie is all about it! It's a comedy first and foremost, and while the title is saucy, the story is a throwback to tamer times that celebrate cute cheesecake pinups and the whimsy of vaudeville.

At the time of this writing, *Cabaret of the Dead* is available to stream on Pluto, Roku, and Screambox. You can watch the trailer on Vimeo.

A fully illustrated, full-color special hardcover of this novelization is also available. That edition contains the complete screenplay/script, as well as behind-the-scenes photographs taken during the filming of *Cabaret of the Dead.*

Special thanks to my constant beta reader, Linda Rose!

Lastly, if you liked this book, please kindly rate and review… indie authors depend on word of mouth (or word of fingertips, as the case may be). Thank you!

About the Author

Staci Layne Wilson adores writing about herself in the third person and playing with her pet Dumbo Rats. She is an L.A. native who enjoys traffic, wildfires, and earthquakes—but since her move to Las Vegas, she's learned to love 110-degree summers, drive-thru wedding chapels, and casinos that still reek of the Rat Pack's cigars. She has been a professional writer since the age of twelve when she was hired as a columnist for a national magazine. When she's not writing books, she's making movies (*Cabaret of the Dead*, *The Ventures: Stars on Guitars*, *The Second Age of Aquarius*, and *Dark House of the Mannequins*).